Faro Sent His Horse Slowly Ahead,

silently urging it to be damned careful about where it put its feet. His right boot swung over the edge of the trail, the left from time to time scraped the near-vertical cliff face. The rock was weathered, and disposed in broken slabs creating miniature caves. Though now in shadow, it had absorbed the sun's heat through the morning hours, and was now radiating the warmth it had collected.

Suddenly, he heard a shrill cry from the rear of the line. He swiveled his head. Brown and his horse were clearly in view. Brown swayed in the saddle, clutching his throat. Then Faro saw something thin whip out from the crevices in the cliff and hit at Brown's cheek. At the same time he was aware of a buzzing sound . . . it increased in volume. Faro registered a stirring and writhing in the deep shadows of the narrow valves in the cliff face . . .

There was no staying here, with God knows how many rattlers waking . . . "Ride like hell!" he called, and spurred his horse.

Books by Zeke Masters

Published by POCKET BOOKS

Most Pocket Books are available at special quantity discounts for bulk purchases for sales promotions, premiums or fund raising. Special books or book excerpts can also be created to fit specific needs.

For details write or telephone the office of the Vice President of Special Markets, Pocket Books, 1230 Avenue of the Americas, New York, New York 10020. (212) 245-6400, ext. 1760.

#23

A ZEKE MASTERS WESTERN

LONG ODDS

PUBLISHED BY POCKET BOOKS NEW YORK

Another *Original* publication of POCKET BOOKS

POCKET BOOKS, a Simon & Schuster division of
GULF & WESTERN CORPORATION
1230 Avenue of the Americas, New York, N.Y. 10020

ISBN: 0-671-45182-0

First Pocket Books printing December, 1982

10 9 8 7 6 5 4 3 2 1

POCKET and colophon are registered trademarks
of Simon & Schuster.

Printed in the U.S.A.

Author's Note

For the sake of the narrative, several geographical improbabilities have been introduced in the description of the Colorado River area in this work. There is a precedent for this practice; the writer of an earlier adventure, to which this owes much, did the same with the eastern Mediterranean.

ZM

LONG ODDS

Chapter 1

Faro Blake's face brightened as he exposed the card he had just cut from the deck, the jack of spades. Sam Volksmacht would have to stretch his run of luck considerably to beat that, he thought. Sam had won against Porky James—king over a two—and a bunch of others, and the run had to be about at an end.

Volksmacht's hand hovered over the deck, the fingers clenched in to make the cut, then exposed the chosen card. The queen of hearts.

"Shit," Faro said. The odds against beating a jack were ten to three; on one cut, that should have been a safe proposition, especially with Sam's steady series of wins. Well, now I am about to go get my ass shot off over something I don't give a damn about, since I give my word to Sam I'd abide by how the cut went. A bet's a bet, and if you don't abide by it, you might's well go into the ribbon-clerking line, for there won't be the meanest card fancier that'll care to get into a game with a man that don't back up what he says he'll do.

So here you are, Blake, locked into a expedition that'll likely get you corpsed. And all along of listening to a woman when it comes to money. . . .

"You got to admit it makes sense," Nell Garvin had said. "It's plain foolish to carry all that cash around with you without you got a need for it at the moment. That kind of money, the thing is to keep the best part of it in a safe place until as you want it to sit in on a big game. Just go toting it on you, and you take a chance on some bummer taking it off of you at gunpoint or so."

"I can take care of myself," Faro said, irritated. It seemed to him that this was a hell of a time to discuss his finances. He was spraddled on the disordered coverlet of Nell's bed, with Nell warmly impaled on him, looking at him through the damp tangle of her loosened hair. He squinted past her pendant breasts, down the taut but rounded belly, shiny with the sweat of their recent exertions, to the mingled patches of hair—his a shade darker and coarser than hers—that masked where they were joined. Nell's nipples were still—or again—jutting stiffly. Onliest woman I know, he thought, that can get in heat talking about money.

"Well, sure," Nell said. "I don't question that for a instant, no, sir. Only there was that time up in Wyoming, I recollect, when you was carrying Long Johnny Jaeger's stake, and got it took off you. And them banknotes back in Centennial year, that turned up missing on that train. And them is only the things I know about first-hand. Wouldn't surprise me, the last some years, you been cleaned out of what you had on you more times than one."

"There is that," Faro said, recalling a few occasions that he had never cared to tell Nell about. When their random itineraries—his as a professional gambler, hers as a successful madam—threw them together, he didn't have all that much inclination to reminisce about the dumber things that had happened to him since their last meeting. It was usually a fast hello, maybe a drink or so in the parlor of whatever house she was operating wherever it was, and then upstairs and to bed. It had been that way pretty much ever since they'd met, over in New Mexico—a long time before, that was, but Nell had by God damn few signs of wear and tear on her. . . .

"Twelve and a few hundreds beyond that is maybe more than I ought to have in my pockets," he said thoughtfully, "being as there ain't nothing I heared of going on just now that calls for such. Could be a idea to travel lighter. If I can't hit a place with a thousand or so in hand and operate with that, I expect I shouldn't be in my trade. So there's ten thousand I could do without until there come up a real big game I wanted to get into."

Coming into Yuma with only a modest stake, Faro had set up his faro bank in a local saloon and had had the luck to attract the patronage of one Homer Tabard, a man of extremely clouded reputation from somewhere north in Arizona Territory. Tabard had been down to Yuma on a spree, dividing his time and resources between womanizing—which, Faro supposed, accounted for his nickname of "Three-Balls"—and gambling. It was rumored that what he was spending was the proceeds of rustling, extortion and hired murder. A lot was whispered about Tabard, but his obvious friendship with local and territorial—and even federal—politicians kept the whispers from becoming shouts. Whether he was or was not a kingpin outlaw, Tabard, a massive man of about fifty, was a dedicated and luckless gambler. In two nights he had impassively dropped close to $12,000 "bucking the tiger" at Faro's bank. At the end of the second evening's play, he had merely said, "Asked around about you. Got the name of running a square game, no special dealing boxes or such into it. So it looks like I lost fair. Good, otherwise you'd be a dead man. Any road, there's more where that came from."

Faro had briefly wondered how many stolen and rebranded cattle, how many looted stages, or how many drygulchings had contributed to his winnings, but had decided that it was none of his business.

"But it don't set well with me to put all that into a bank," he told Nell. "I don't read the papers much, but whenas I do, seems to me one of the fuckers is always failing, and the folks that had their money in it can exercise their constitutional rights to go piss up a rope."

Nell's white poodle bitch, Claire, jumped on him, whining and scratching. Faro sighed and kicked the dog deftly away. Claire was a pest, but Nell seemed to like her.

"Don't have to keep it in an account," Nell said softly, leaning closer to him and brushing his chest with one stiff nipple. "I been checking around with banks and such since I got here—there's some business things I want to talk to you about later, that I been finding out about—and there's another way to handle it."

Faro pushed aside a twinge of unease about Nell's "business things" and asked, "What's that?"

"Safe-deposit box," Nell breathed, letting her hair trail across his face. "Not part of the bank's assets. You just take anything you value, and hire a box to put it in, and you can put it in when you want and take it out when you want."

"Hey," Faro said, breathing a little hoarsely as Nell flexed her thighs to rise and fall gently on him. "Might be a idea. Something you set some store by . . ." He felt his erection swell to fullness again, sliding in Nell. ". . . you just put it in . . ." He arched himself to drive upwards.

"Hahhh," Nell murmured.

". . . and take it out whenas you want . . ."

Nell gave a soft, complaining gasp and reached down to guide him into her again.

". . . and put it back in, and then take it out and put it in and . . ."

Later, he lit a cheroot and puffed smoke at the ceiling. "I just now learned more about banking than I ever knowed before," he said. "If I'd of had such instruction in it when I was a pup, I expect I'd be able to give J. P. Morgan cards, spade and little casino by now and come out ahead. Okay, I'll put ten thousand of what I've got into the, uh, box, and hit out with the rest, next day or so. Expect to be working not too far from here for a month or what, so it won't be no bother to get on the cars and come down, should I need it."

"Good," Nell said drowsily. "Take you around to the First Territorial tomorrow, set it up. We can get at the business stuff I was talking of, same time."

"Oh, yeah. What kind of business stuff is that?"

"Mrrw," Nell said, and began breathing heavily and evenly as she relaxed against him.

With his last vestiges of wakefulness, Faro stubbed out the cheroot and wondered if Nell had been mumbling "tomorrow" or giving a shorter purr to indicate that the business had to do with cathouses, which would make sense, given that she was a house-catkeeper, no, shit, hatcousekeeper, thass not it neither, feels mighty good skrooched up against her like this, cats or not. . . .

As it turned out, both of his guesses were right.

Nell's business affairs and her proposals for Faro's role in them at first alarmed him when she revealed them to him the next day. "We done some things together in the past," he said, "and I got to admit you done your part like a man in some rough places, and we know just about how much to trust each other, and such. But signing on as partners, with it all wrote out and legal, well, hell, Nell, that I never studied on, and it seems to fit some tight about the shoulders and waist."

"I'm aware of that, God knows," Nell said with a touch of acidity Faro did not understand. "But this isn't a real partnership, Blake. I'll own everything and I'll run everything and I'll keep every damn penny of profit. What I need's your name—any man's name, for that matter—on the partnership papers, that's all. I mean to buy Eighteen Ithaca Street—" This, Faro recalled after a brief moment of incomprehension, was the address of the premises Nell was renting. "—and now that I been looking around Yuma, I got me a fancy to buy up some other property and cash in when the prices go up. It's a shitty town, but the Territorial pen brings in a lot of trade, lawyers, politicians, outlaws and such, and it's got the smell of a place that's going to grow. I got the notion I could make a heap of money in a little while, buying right and selling when it comes time to move on. But the thing is, a lone woman, she don't get taken serious enough when it comes to business. Bank loans and leases and such, first question the fellows ask is: What's your husband's assets, or your partner's? I done a little sniffing around, and it's damn clear that I can buy and sell and bargain

about how I want, so long's I'm acting for a partnership that's got a man to it. Guess they figure that if I
fuck up, the male end of the act will beat me up or
something."

"Hell, you got a better head for business than any
man I ever see," Faro protested. "That don't hardly
seem fair."

"You looking for fair, go buy a ticket to heaven or
hell," Nell said sourly. "Them places got a name for
treating the inmates just like they deserve, no better
and no worse. In Arizona Territory, and about any
place I ever been or heard tell of, the notion don't
apply."

Finally persuaded, Faro signed the partnership papers Nell proffered and suggested a separate agreement renouncing any responsibility or claim on profits.
"Don't need that, Blake," Nell said. "I know you
wouldn't do me dirty."

"Hey," Faro said, "ain't you trusting me kind of
far?"

"Not much. You know damn well that if you did, I'd
bite your balls off and stuff them down your throat."

On the northbound train out of Yuma that afternoon, with $10,000 of his stake safely (he hoped)
deposited in the First Territorial, and a little over
$2,000 nested in his brass-fitted leather "tool case,"
along with his gambling paraphernalia and his emer-
gency armament—a double-barreled shotgun with the
stock and barrels sawed off so that it was little larger
than an old-fashioned dragoon pistol and could easily
be concealed in a special sling under his coat in case of
trouble—Faro considered Nell's comment. From her,
it was about the same as another woman saying
"Thanks for the favor, and have a wonderful trip." No
denying it, Nell had her own kind of flavor.

No denying, too, that she'd been right about it being sensible to keep the bulk of his money where it'd be ready when he needed it.

Faro held this opinion for just over two months. Sixty-two days later, he was watching Sam Volksmacht cut just one card higher than he had, and cursing Nell's advice, Nell herself, and most of all, the misguided impulse that had made him go along with her.

Chapter 2

After travels that had taken him to a dozen towns in the two months since he had left Yuma, it was in Flagstaff that Faro heard of Sam Volksmacht's farewell party. The journey had swelled his stake pleasantly, rail travelers being notoriously prone to games of chance to pass the time. He had not had to employ any of his special skills or any of the devices, such as the sleeve holdout, the shiners and the markers, nested in his tool case; his familiarity with poker, the preferred en route game, and with the reactions of opposing players, was enough to give him all the advantage he needed.

In Flagstaff, which he had passed through only a few times before, he set up his bank at the Atheneum Café, the town's liveliest saloon and entertainment establishment. He anticipated about a week or ten days' operation there before moving on, and calculated that he would come close to doubling his stake in that time.

It was something he had to admit, to know that he had a big chunk of money waiting for him down in the ass-end of the Territory, and that whatever he came out ahead with could be added onto it if he wanted. Go on like this, Blake, he told himself, and you're gonna set up to be a capitalist, which you'll be able to buy and sell houses and lots and such, just like Nell Garvin.

On his second night at the Atheneum, Faro was approached by Toad Dabney. Dabney was an old-line gambler, seasoned on the Mississippi before the war. Faro remembered him from his youth as a crony of his father, A. B. Blake, who was then running his games on a succession of sidewheelers, and, later, as an occasionally encountered colleague on the western frontier. Faro had heard the name before meeting the man, and had asked his father, "How come they call him Toad, Pa?" "You ever see him, you wouldn't of asked," A. B. had said.

Now, meeting the squat man with the bulging eyes and wide, thin mouth once again, Faro was reminded forcefully of the old days on the Mississippi. The river had been his home for eight years, between ten and eighteen, when he was ill-advisedly shoehorned into college. It had been a good life, but, no matter how much traveling he had done in the year since, none of it was quite like moving up and down the mighty body of water. Things had changed on the Mississippi, though; the riverboats were no longer the gamblers' haven that they had been, and there was no going back.

"Hey, Blake," Dabney said.

"Toad," Faro said. "How you been?"

"Well enough," Dabney said. "But not's well's I expect to be from Thursday on."

"How come Thursday's such a tonic?" Faro asked.

Dabney's naturally wide mouth extended itself.

"Sam's party," he said. "Girls on tap, likewise booze and food 'til hell wouldn't have it. And—"

"Whose which?" Faro cut in.

"Sam Volksmacht's, you know," Dabney said. "Must've heard about it."

"I ain't," Faro said. "Just got in yesterday, rested up at the hotel after three days on the cars, come over here to set up. What's old Sam partying about and where's he at?"

Volksmacht, he recalled, was an old-time saloon keeper who made a specialty of presenting an unusual variety of entertainment in his places, sometimes presenting top eastern vaudeville acts that were touring the west. Almost the first sign of a boom in some hitherto obscure town—after the arrival of the whores and gamblers—was the appearance of Sam and his staff and the opening of his saloon-theater, in a tent if necessary. And when Sam's place closed its doors, or flaps, it was a signal that the boom had passed, and the town was ready to turn ghost, or slide into respectability. He had always been hospitable to gamblers, demanding only a modest percentage of their take and insisting on honest games. Faro had run a few banks in Sam's saloons in various towns, but had found that the constant entertainment offered too much distraction and tended to deter the serious players.

"Made his pile, Sam has," Dabney said, "and means to retire. Going to go back to Germany, Sam is, and live like a lord. Maybe even become one, grease a couple palms at the Kaiser's court, and it ain't that hard to get at least some bitty title, Sam says. Tickles me to think of what all them Dutchmen'll make of Lady Sam, or whatever they'll call her."

"Sam's hitched?" Faro asked.

Dabney nodded. "Just a while back, to that Mex woman he's been partnering informal for the last whatever years, La Canasta." When Faro claimed ignorance of the attachment, Dabney continued, "Singer he hired on for one of his shows, then decided to continue the engagement on other terms. Ain't hard to see why—about the handsomest woman I ever seen. Elena Gutierrez, that's her straight monicker. Caught her act once, she come out with a basket full of fruit on her head, and sang like an angel, Mex songs, and every man in the place not knowing whether to watch for the basket to fall off, listen to her voice, or just plain feast his eyes on her."

Faro dug in his memory for what he retained of Spanish from his postwar years in Mexico, and said, *"Canasta* means basket, seems to me—the balancing stuff, that's why they call her that, huh?"

"The name come first," Dabney said. "Down in Old Mexico, *canasta's* a nickname for a woman's inward privates, and it seems that Elena used to give hers steadier employment than you'd care to believe. When she commenced to have ambitions to work standing up, and turned to singing, she decided to trade on the reputation she'd built up down there, and worked the basket into her act. She'd throw the fruit into the audience at the end, then wind up by pulling a banana out, real slow, and then she'd peel it and eat it. Not a dry crotch in the house."

"This party," Faro said.

"Well, old Sam's decided to go out in style. He's over in some dinky place on the Colorado called Tornup, where there's been a good silver strike, and he's doing his usual business. And now that the lode looks like pinching out, he's decided to call it a day, call in what he's got, and hit out for Prooshia. And before he goes, he means to throw a wing-ding that'll be talked of up to at least nineteen-thirty.

"Fifty-some years is a long time to recollect a party," Faro said.

"Them that's there will have it in mind to their dying day," Dabney said earnestly. "Girls, liquor, food, entertainment, whatever you've a mind for, and not a penny to spend. Of course," he went on, "as Sam's put out a general call for all and sundry that's ever worked in one of his places to come and freeload on him, at least the ones that's in traveling distance, there'll be fellows like you and me, so I expect there'll be some good poker sessions, not to mention craps and whatever. There'll be money changing hands at a considerable rate, I don't doubt, and it's best to go in there armed for bear. But Sam's not even taking his usual cut, and everything's free, bar whatever you choose to wager."

"And I take it," Faro said, "that thisyer's a general invite? I mean, I don't got to of got a engraved piece of pasteboard in the mail to qualify?"

"Open house," Toad Dabney said. "You done business with Sam in the past, you're welcome. There'll be fancy ladies, old barkeeps, entertainers, gamblers, whatall. And, for sure, me."

Faro had already come to the conclusion that Flagstaff was not a place he would find pleasant or profitable for long—on his way next week at the latest, he had decided before the first evening's play was half done. No harm in advancing the date of departure a little. "Me too," he said.

Arriving with Dabney two days later at the site of Sam Volksmacht's latest American venture, Faro found that his companion's account of the scope of the party had not been exaggerated. In the vast, rambling building where Volksmacht headquartered—a hotel catering to consumptives that some believer in the virtues of Arizona's dry air had erected and soon abandoned, before the silver strike—he found what seemed like a good third of the men and women he had encountered during the last ten years. Nell Garvin wasn't in Tornup, of course, nor Doc Prentiss, but Bigfoot Bertha was, and Knifelips Hogan, and Jake Harington, and Blinky Castle, along with a lot of others—a fine mix of whores, gamblers, gunmen, sports and general drifters, all quartered in reasonable comfort in the Sparta House's considerable complement of bedrooms.

"Heydee, Blake," Sam Volksmacht said, greeting him. " 'Member you from Dodge and Hayes, good t'see you. M'lady here'll show you where you're to lodge."

Following La Canasta up the Sparta House's stairs, Faro could see why she had appealed to her clientele, as well as to Sam Volksmacht. Even swathed in all the layers of cloth and whalebone that custom called for, she had a shape and movement that made a man give serious thought to the notion of grabbing her by the waist, pushing her down onto the treads, hoisting her skirts, and getting at what was underneath. He didn't, he considered, even particularly desire her, but there was no denying that being around her would get any man's prod about as stiff as it could be. It was the opposite of jumping into an icy mountain lake, that would shrink up a man's cock and balls the size of a walnut—no matter what your opinions were, the physical reaction was there.

Sam Volksmacht's party lived up to Toad Dabney's advance billing and surpassed it. From late morning to early morning, there was everything anyone could want in the way of food, drink, diversion and company of the opposite sex, and no bills to keep in mind.

"This's going to do me for a lifetime," Toad Dabney declared, the evening of the day of his and Faro's arrival at Volksmacht's realm. "I am going to guard my health and turn to Fletcherizing and other rational courses so's I can go on remembering this until at least I am a hundred—it'd be a damn waste to die sooner and lose the recollection of it. Hey, hold back with the teeth there, honey. Velvet lips, that's it."

Watching a plump blonde girl browse enthusiastically on Toad's surprisingly ample private parts, while he himself was enjoying an inventive brunette—one of a troupe of contortionists that Sam Volksmacht had summoned to his farewell—Faro agreed that the occasion would linger in memory. There were five couples altogether—and mostly in the altogether—and one trio in the large, sunny room on the second floor. Most of them were consciously or involuntarily moving in time to the rhythm of Blinky Castle's fiddle. The blind singer was seated in the corner, and at the moment giving a spirited rendering of "Shenandoah," with improvised lyrics.

> *The trapper's prick got hard and harder,*
> *Way-hay, you rolling river,*
> *But then she says, "Here comes my father!"*
> *Away, we're bound away*
> *'Crost the wide Missouri.*

"Yo, Blinky," a man called, not slowing his efforts with a statuesque redhead spraddled on a sofa with one foot planted on the wall and the other on the floor, "don't it gall you not to be able to see all this goin' on?"

"I'm shy one sense," the fiddler said, continuing to play, but more softly, "but all that means is that the others is honed up beyond the ordinary. Know any man I ever met by his voice, an' that includes you, Parrish Tabard, an' can tell what's goin' on any place just by the sound of it. An' what I'm hearin' don't leave me any deprived, I'll tell you. Can imagine everything clear as crystal, what you and Blake and Dabney and them is up to. Only thing, I expect I'm seein' the ladies and you as bein' some better-lookin' than what you are. I'll tell you, just from what I'm hearin', my rod's about to pop my trouser buttons, stiff enough so's I could use it on my fiddle 'stead of a bow."

"Sounds interesting," the slight girl who was part of the threesome on the floor in the corner opposite Blinky said. She detached herself from the man and the other woman, walked a little unsteadily across the room to the fiddler, knelt in front of him and worked at his trouser front as he lifted the fiddle over her head and continued sawing away. She took him into her mouth and began moving up and down. "High damn!" Blinky said delightedly, and changed his tune to the jog-trot of "The Yellow Rose of Texas."

Faro, now pistoning in time to the faster Ta-tum-ta-tum-ta-ta-ta-tum of the song, turned toward Dabney and said, "Parrish Tabard?"

"Old Three-Balls's son," Dabney panted, holding his girl's head firmly in place as he thrust into her mouth with the beat Blinky was setting. "Said to be an owlhoot, like his old man, but he's been a good customer of Sam's, and up here there ain't much store set by which side of the law a man's on so long's he don't trouble those he's doing business with."

Sam Volksmacht and his Elena appeared in the doorway of the room. "That's right, enjoy," Sam called. "By jing, Elena, take a look. Don't think we'll see such goings on in Potsdam, eh?"

La Canasta silently surveyed the revelers, her

glance conveying a cool appreciation of the abilities of all concerned. Though she was fully clothed, and at a distance, her presence excited Faro more than the woman he was occupied with, and it seemed to him that his penis swelled substantially beyond its normal erect state as he continued thrusting. The woman under him gasped and moved enthusiastically. He wondered what her reaction would be if she knew that the sudden increase in her pleasure was due to his being appraised in action by another woman.

The lean, dark man Blinky had identified as Parrish Tabard stared hungrily at La Canasta. His body was suddenly rigid and still as the redhead writhed beneath him, then scissored her wide-flung legs around him and whooped hoarsely. Tabard gave a brief twitch, then relaxed, his gaze still fixed on the woman in the doorway. Not until she and Volksmacht had left did the tension seem to flow out of him, letting him lie limply on the gasping redhead.

Now that fellow just come in a little while ago, way I recall, Faro thought, and likely this here was his first sight of the lady. For sure, it took him strong. . . .

As he finished with his girl, quickening the pace of his strokes when he felt his climax coming on, his mind was for once not on what he was doing. Tabard had the look of a hardcase, all right, a man who'd take what he wanted, and damn the torpedoes. He smelled trouble on the way.

"Doubt it considerably," Toad Dabney said a few minutes later. He and Faro, once more dressed, were taking the stairs down to the first floor for some badly needed drink and food. "Sam's had experience in handling fellows who try to get at his woman. Prime goods like that, she draws 'em without even meaning to, and Sam's learned how to discourage 'em some forceful. Does it polite when he can, rough when he has to, up to and past bonebreaking. Tabard's tough, but he's shrewd, and he's not going to buck the odds by making a try for Sam's woman in Sam's house, with a dozen or what of Sam's friends around. If he's got a hard-on for her, well, there's plenty of others around for him to stick it into. And if he wants to pretend it's La Canasta he's screwing, that's his business."

He brightened as he entered the large room where the drink and food were laid out. "Looks like a good game going, over there in the corner, a nice, sizeable pot on the table. After we get ourselves fueled up, let's go show them fellows how poker's really played."

How poker is really played, Faro reminded himself a few hours later, is that some win and some lose. And the man that don't forget everything but the game, why, that man's likely to wind up the loser. Shit, why'd I let myself stew about that Tabard and Sam's woman, keep checking around to see if he'd showed up here yet . . . ?

"That does it for me, gents," he said, rising from the table. "I'm Tap City, for fair. Been instructive, I'll tell you."

"Bad luck, Blake," one of the winning players said.

Faro shook his head. "Bad poker playing, thass what it was, and no getting around it."

"Everybody hits an off day," another player said. "You want to sit in tomorrow, we'd be glad to take your markers."

"Kind of you," Faro said. "But I don't give such, nor take 'em when I can help it. I play for money only, and not no marbles or chalk."

Dabney, also a heavy loser in the session, left the table with him. "Square game, far's I saw," he said.

"It was," Faro said. "No matter how much I screwed up, I wasn't so far out of things that I wouldn't of noticed any fast work. Anyhow, a game with fellows that's in the trade, it'd be plain stupid to pull anything funny. Whatever you tried, likely the man that invented it'd be sitting across the table from you."

"Right," Dabney agreed. "Same like what I said about Parrish Tabard. He'd have to be crazy to do anything about La Canasta, never mind what kind of cravings for her he's got. Think Sam's noticed anything about that?"

"Feel like asking him, you can," Faro muttered, nudging Dabney. "Here he is now."

Volksmacht greeted them genially. "Having yourselves a good time, boys? Plenty of everything?"

"About every appetite I knowed I got has been satisfied about every way I can think of," Faro said. "This is the completest wing-ding I ever seen, and I got to thank you for it."

"More to come," Volksmacht said proudly. "Tonight, Elena sings for us all. Her last performance in America—after tonight, she sings for me only. Be sure to be in the back room about midnight."

"Would think she'd be some tuckered by then," Toad Dabney said. "From what I recall, the lady don't spare herself when she's putting on a show."

"Oh, she'll be fresh for it," Volksmacht said. "She's upstairs in her room, resting, and I won't wake her up until it's 'most time to get into her costume."

"That will be something," Dabney said. "La Canasta's last show—and free, gratis for nothing, along with everything else you done for us."

Volksmacht shrugged his wide shoulders. "Customers, performers, people I did business with, they're what made me the money I've got, so I figured it made sense to use up a little of it for a good sendoff." He looked shrewdly at the two men. "Even so, looks like it's come out expensive for some. Noticed you fellows leaving the game before it broke up. Get cleaned out, did you?"

"Yeah," Faro said. "I will be spending the rest of the party with nothing to do but eat, drink, fornicate and be entertained. Toad'll have to stake me for the coach ride back to Flagstaff—once I'm there I can wire a friend in Yuma for some money I got there."

"How much did you drop?"

"Two thousand and change."

Volksmacht's lips pursed in a silent whistle of surprise. He turned to Dabney. "And you?"

"Not as much, but enough for tonight, for damn sure—just over a thousand."

Volksmacht shook his head. "I never could understand that, what makes people gamble. I took lots of risk in my businesses, but always on something I could have a chance at controlling. I remember telling your father, Blake—you recollect, A. B. and I were pretty fair pals back when I was starting out, before the war—I remember telling him that he'd always be losing back what he won, so long as he stuck to that line of work. Me, I may not always make as much as I want to, but I mostly hung onto it. See you later—don't forget, midnight in the back room."

By midnight, the inhabitants of Volksmacht's vast house—guests, servants, entertainers—were indeed assembled as invited. But the vocalizing that riveted their attention was not the renowned voice of La Canasta but Sam Volksmacht's enraged bellow.

"That sonofabitch Tabard—the bastard's kidnapped Elena!"

Chapter 3

Sam Volksmacht, glaring wildly and, Faro noticed, looking close to ten years older than he had a few hours ago, stilled the babble of noise from the crowd by yelling, "Shut the fuck up, goddammit!"

He turned to the dazed-looking girl he had dragged into the room, moments before the performance had been scheduled to begin, and said, "Maria-Antonia, you tell them, just like you told it to me."

The girl was slightly built, olive-skinned, dark-haired, and outfitted in a black cotton dress with a lace-edged white apron—the uniform of a lady's maid, which was a damned strange kind of person to find out here in the badlands, Faro thought. On the other hand, Sam Volksmacht and his lady were the sort of people who made their own rules for how things were.

"*Sí*," the girl quavered. "It was about eight, half-past, *la señorita* was sleeping, and I was sitting in a chair alongside her bed, I had a pillowcase I was, um, you know, sewing lace onto the edges. Is very fine

29

lace, the sisters in Toledo, they make it, and *la señorita*, she—"

"Maria-Antonia!" Volksmacht grated. "Forget the lace!"

"Oh. Oh, *sí*. Well, I was . . . doing what I was doing, and then I hear the door open behind me. I think it is *el señor* coming in to wake up *la señorita* the way he does sometimes, you know, *los pantalones* open and his—"

"Maria-Antonia!"

"—so I didn't look up, but then I saw this man, a man I didn't know, and he was holding a gun, and he said, like very quiet, 'Squick and I kill you,' then he go to *la señorita* and shake her by the shoulder and wake her up, and he say, 'I am Porsh Dobardo, and you are going to be Missus Porsh Dobardo or the next best thing, or you are going to be dead. When I saw you this afternoon, when I was in that room upstairs—*Señor* Folgamaga," the girl said, interrupting herself, "did the gorls you asked to clin that place get to it? You 'member, you said it had to be . . ." One look at Sam Volksmacht's apoplectic expression caused her to break off the question and continue hurriedly. "Anyhow, he said, 'I am going to prod you four ways from the ace, to start with, them I am going to' . . . well, he said what he was going to do, you know? And *la señorita* was trying to hit him, and he had his hand over her mouth so she couldn't yell out, and he put the gun to her head, and he made me tie her with the scarves she had in her wardrobe, and tie a scarf around her mouth to keep her quiet, and then he said, 'Good enough,' and then he stepped around behind me and then I felt this big pen in my head, and the next thing I know, *el señor* is waking me up in the room and asking me what happen. And all I know what happen is just what I said."

"Found Maria-Antonia lying on the floor in Elena's room," Volksmacht said heavily. "Bedclothes all in a tangle, things upset—and no Elena." He paused, his face contorted and his teeth grinding against each other. "I woke her up, got the story out of her. No question, it seems to me, that that cocksucker Tabard has kidnapped her, and decked the girl here with his gunbutt to keep her quiet for long enough to make his getaway! I had the stables checked as soon as I could make sense out of what Maria-Antonia had to say, and Tabard's horse is gone."

"Likely he'll be well on his way to Devil's Den by now," said Knifelips Hogan, who had sat in on Faro's disastrous poker session. "Where's that?" Faro asked Toad Dabney.

"Three-Balls's hideout out in the badlands," Dabney said. "A kind of collection of canyons, that there ain't but one way in to. The old man's been holed up there for years, made about a whole town of his own out of it, and no way to prise him out without you was to drop a regiment of infantry on him out of balloons. And Knifelips Hogan should know. It's said he put in some time with the Tabards, years back, and since done some town-taming for places that needed it and weren't all that choosy about the man that done it or the ways it was done."

Faro nodded. He was aware of Hogan's reputation. It wasn't uncommon for a man who'd spent a spell as an outlaw to turn his coat and work the other side of the fence. Either way, it worked out to risking his hide and using his gun for the party that paid him, and there were more than a few police chiefs and town marshals who had unimpeccable criminal credentials. Hogan, he remembered, had been one of those who'd come away from the poker table with a lot less than he'd sat down with.

"Four hours on the trail, and knowing the country the way he does, old Parrish's likely got hisself a good part of the way there already," Hogan continued. He was a leathery-skinned man of anywhere between thirty and fifty, with a calmly dangerous air to him. When he was not speaking, his mouth seemed almost to disappear, being visible only as a thin line a third of the way between his sharp nose and chin. "Parrish's about the best there is, when it comes to finding your way around this kind of cut-up land in the dark. Even riding double with the lady behind him, I don't doubt he'll be making better time than anyone else could alone."

"Nice to know my lady's in good hands," Sam Volksmacht said heavily. "Now, let's get going out after the fucker!"

Knifelips Hogan shook his head. "Like I said, he's got a start, and he knows the trails, where we'd have to cast about for 'em, and no way of knowing, in the dark, which was right. We could wind up headed for Oregon or Texas, come morning. No, you can figure on it, he'll be all the way to the Den long before anybody after him could get above halfway there."

Volksmacht ground his teeth. "All right, we'll follow him! Go right in there and get her back and hang Parrish Tabard up by his balls!"

There was a silence in the room. Hogan broke it by saying, thoughtfully, "We . . ."

"Now, damn it all," Sam Volksmacht said, "you fellows have had the biggest time of your lives on me, you're my guests and old pals and whatall, and my lady's been stolen right while you were all here to see it! It stands to reason you'll side me to get her back!"

"The south stage for Flagstaff, what time's that leave, Toad?" Faro muttered to Dabney. "I got a feeling this party's over, and that's the way I as soon leave it."

"Me too. Late morning, I think. I'll stake you to the fare, okay?"

Hogan shook his head. "You ain't been in the Den, Sam. I have, when I was . . . well, doing a special assignment I can't talk about."

"Tucson National Bank, back in '75," Toad Dabney whispered. "A Tabard job for sure, and somebody with a slit for a mouth riding with him, though there was never enough witnesses to make it stick. For sure, he can't talk about it."

"And I'll tell you," Hogan went on, "there's just no way to get into the Den. Was Tabard holed up in some ranch house or what, you could work out how to get some men in place on whatever high ground there was, find cover, and smoke him out. But the Den's got only the one way in, a crack in the rockwall that's no wider'n two horses, and one or two men with enough ammunition can stand off an army there. And I know for a fact that old Three-Balls has sentries out there every living hour of the day and night. Once every year or so, there's some lawman that figures he's got a beef with the Tabards, and goes up to the Den, and then comes back with about half the posse wrapped in blankets and slung over their horses, and boom times ahead for the undertakers. And nothing ever done about it from higher up, what with old Three-Balls's connections in high places, like they say."

"How late in the morning?" Faro asked Toad Dabney. He sympathized with Sam Volksmacht, but what was going on was none of his business, and this looked like a good setup to be away from, soon.

"Ten, eleven," Dabney said.

"Be an idea to be down there by six, maybe," Faro

said. "I don't care for early rising, but I don't think it's a good idea to stay here much after first light, or Sam might get the notion to pass his own draft act."

"Well, damn, this is a time when a man finds out what friends are for," Volksmacht said, surveying his audience with disgust. "Okay, I ain't ever freeloaded yet, and I won't start now. A dozen men, that's got some nerve and some wits, that's what I need to go up there and study out a way to get into the Den and get Elena out of it, and that bastard's balls to boot. A thousand dollars a head, that's what I'm offering."

"Count on me, Sam!"

Volksmacht looked at the speaker with irritation. "Glad you got the sand for it, but unless you got a plan to sniff your way in, I don't see you'd be much use, Blinky."

In spite of the fact that a thousand dollars was a good deal more than some of those present might see in a year, there were no further takers of Volksmacht's offer after the blind fiddler. "Thing is, Sam, it ain't our quarrel," Knifelips Hogan said, "and the pay don't make it so. Maybe something might could be done, was you to get a bunch up to the Den, but it ain't ever worked yet."

"Huh," Volksmacht said. He studied his motley array of guests for a moment, then said, "Lots of you fellows are gamblers—some of you professionals, some just sit in for fun. All right, I'll tell you straight out, I'm going to trade on that, though you all know I'm not one and never have been. Now, I've kept track of the games you've been in here, and I know about who's won and lost how much. I'm not getting a percentage of the pots any more, but it's come to be a habit with me over the years. So here it is. I'll make up what you've lost or sweeten your winnings. All you got to do is cut cards with me. You cut high, you take your money and go. Cut low, you get the cash all the same, but you agree to come along with me to help get Elena away from that bastard Tabard."

There was a stirring and exchanges of glances among the assembly. "Damn," Toad Dabney said thoughtfully. "One thing to take wages to go get shot at by them Tabards, another to have a chance of getting back what I lost for free."

"And listen," Volksmacht went on. "It won't be one of these posse things, everyone going out with some hardtack and a canteen. We can't follow the bastard close, not at night and with the start he's got, so we might as well do it in style—that's my way, as you all know damn well. Supplies enough for ten days, booze included. And if we haven't been able to bring it off by then, why then, the job's off, and I live with what I have to, and you go off with your money and no hard feelings. If there's enough of us, we can maybe starve them out, make old Three-Balls see sense, and it needn't come to fighting. An excursion, like. And . . . hey, you girls! Goldie, Winnie! A thousand each, you willing to come along? Cook, serve out drinks, and whatever?"

The two hired girls that Volksmacht had called out to looked at each other, then nodded. Faro remembered that Winnie had made up his bed that morning, after having helped him disarrange it mightily. If Goldie was anything like her, there'd be enough "whatever" to go around among a dozen men, easy.

"So how about it?" Volksmacht called. "Anybody's willing to chance their luck, just come to my office—first room on the right at the top of the stairs. I'll be there."

He turned and strode from the room.

Knifelips Hogan was the first to stir after their host's departure. "Hell, I lost more'n I care to. Gettin' it back, and only the fifty-fifty chance I'll have to do somethin' for it, I don't believe I'll pass that up."

He left by the door Volksmacht had used. "What d'you think?" Dabney asked Faro.

"Dunno. For me, it beats what Sam come up with first. Instead of a thousand, a sure two and some, and, like Knifelips said, even odds that it don't amount to an enlistment. I'd say it depends on who else is willing and cuts low. If it come out to only Sam and Blinky, going along, I doubt I'd care to take the chance. Less hang back some and see how that goes."

After two minutes, Knifelips Hogan reappeared, a thinly twisted grin on his face. "A two for me, nine for Sam. Which I am also the U.S. Grant for the business, with Sam as Honest Abe. Or Lee and Davis, for them that still holds contrary persuasions. You, Goldie! Keep in mind that as commander-in-chief, I get my breakfast served in bed, and I want my eggs over lightly, and the waitress the same way."

Blinky Castle struck up a slow air on his fiddle.

Now Hogan's the first in the order of battle,
That uses his gun better than other men.
He'll leave all them Tabards to hang and to rattle
Pervided he c'n get inside Devil's Den.

"Thanks a lot, Blinky," Hogan said acidly.

"Well, this is something that's going to be talked of for some damn time," the blind fiddler said. "I got to get set for being able to do a song about it. I know a man over in Tulsa that's got a phonograph. I get all of this down so's I remember it, I c'n have him cut me a cylinder, and folks'll be able to hear about this long after you 'n me 'n the Tabards and all is gone to where the woodbine twineth."

"Well, hey, all right!" a man called in a gurgling voice from the side of the room. "Well, hey, hell, I'll cut against Vomit . . . Volga . . . against Sam. Here goes nothing."

He exited, brandishing a square bottle and then putting its mouth to his lips before vanishing from the oblong of the doorframe. "He's right about that, I'd say," Faro commented to Toad Dabney. "You know him?"

"Soak Backus," Dabney answered. "Comes from a family with big money back East. Fucked up bad when he was younger, so they shot him out here. Give him some cash the first of each month, so long as he stays west of Omaha, but by the second he's drunk up half of it. Last five years, he's probably taken ten thousand dollars' worth of booze on board, and a good chunk of that in Sam's places."

"Just what's wanted to go up against the Tabards," Faro said disgustedly. "Honest to God, old Sam's going about this as crazy as he can."

Backus returned, smiling broadly and waving a fistful of bills. "Voltage cut a two, me, king. So long, suckers, I got my forty-two dollars back, and scot-free into the barbigan. See me through to the firsp of the mump." He weaved over to the corner of the room, braced himself against it, and applied himself to the bottle he still held.

"First two cuts, one win for Sam, one loss," Dabney said.

"Two wins, I'd say," Faro replied, watching Soak Backus slowly slide down the wall.

Slick Phil Bowyer, a confidence man almost in the class of Doc Prentiss, Faro's childhood mentor, was the next to try his luck with Sam Volksmacht. Against Volksmacht's eight, his six earned him a place in the assault party and another verse from Blinky Castle.

*Oh, what will he do now, that poor Slick Phil
    Bowyer?*
He can't work his scams on them Tabards for shit.
*He should of gone t' college and turned out a
    lawyer,*
But now he'll use bullets instead of a writ.

"Last three was losers," Toad Dabney said a few
minutes later. "I got the feeling Sam's at the end of a
run. I'd like the cash back that I lost, and this seems to
be the time to try for it."

Faro debated his situation during Dabney's absence.
Going up against Sam Volksmacht would guarantee
him the return of the sum he had lost during that
disastrous session, and only one chance in two of
having to meet the formidable Tabards under less
pleasant circumstances than he had so far. It would
surely be pretty galling to have to beg funds from Toad
Dabney for the stage trip to Flagstaff—and not at all a
sure thing that Toad, if he lost the cut, would be
forthcoming—and then wire Nell Garvin to get him
some walking-around money. It would also mean that
he'd have to get down to Yuma fast, to get at the safe-
deposit box and repay her, since only he had access to
it.

"Hogan ain't McClellan," Toad Dabney said heavily, sinking onto the chair next to Faro, "that's one
thing on the credit side."

"Meaning which?"

"I cut a nine, Sam the jack, so I am well and truly
recruited for this. When I was a kid, I joined up, and
served under Little Mac, and the sonofabitch farted
around with us so that we never got where we were
supposed to, and got our asses shot off into the bargain. If Hogan maybe knows what he's doing, it puts

him some way ahead of Mac, and maybe I'll live through it."

"You got some cash left, you could just get on the morning stage out to Flagstaff," Faro said. "Sam'll have enough on his plate without worrying about you."

"Shit, Blake," Toad Dabney said. "I made a bet and I lost it. I can't go back on that, unless I want to get into another line of work, and you know that as well's I do. You going to go up and cut against Sam?"

Faro briefly visualized what it would be like to walk from Sam Volksmacht's town to Flagstaff—there was just no point in expecting Toad, in his present circumstances, to advance him stage fare—and said, "Sure." It would be damn satisfying to have his two thousand back, win or lose, and Sam Volksmacht's luck had been variable, with about as many low cuts as high.

Faro wished briefly that he had ignored Nell's advice about keeping the bulk of his money in the safe-deposit box in Yuma. With all that cash in hand, he wouldn't even be thinking about cutting against Sam.

Five minutes later, looking at Sam Volksmacht's queen and his own jack, he was wishing it even more strongly.

It was past two before he got to bed, after Sam had outlined the tasks of the next day. Of the dozen men selected, two—Faro and Porky James—would purchase food, ammunition and booze. Others would see to the hire of horses and rent or purchase a wagon and mules for the transport of the supplies. Faro was figuring out how to grab the job of wagon driver. As far as Faro was concerned, horses were uncomfortable, smelly and unreliable. A man had to be a damn fool to get on top of an animal that would like as not stick its leg in a prairie-dog hole, fall, and roll over on him. He bit into the tip of his cheroot savagely as he realized that the girls, Winnie and Goldie, would likely draw the driving job.

Restless, he rose from his bed and snapped open his tool case. His green felt faro layout, along with the casekeeper and dealing box, were neatly stowed in their places, as were the assortment of "advantage tools"—sleeve holdout, shiners, strippers, nail pricks—he always carried. In the main—and always at the game for which he had been named—Faro played straight, relying on his experience and instinct for the edge he needed. But it made sense to be able to pull about anything, if the occasion called for it. "Doesn't pay to cheat," his father, A. B., had told him long ago, "but it's plain stupid not to know how to."

Well, none of the tools in the case was going to do him much good, coming up against the Tabards. He would have to rely on two other items in the case. The Reid's .38, called by its maker "My Friend," held six slugs and, with its brass-knuckle handle, was an effective blackjack, definitely a close-range weapon. The other was the shotgun he normally carried there. The weapons were effective enough in the situations an itinerant gambler might anticipate, but not all that much use in besieging an outlaw stronghold, unless things got to closer quarters than he cared to think about. A couple of howitzers would be the thing, he thought, but doubted if Sam would be able to find any for rent in Tornup.

He lifted another essential piece of equipment from the case, his flask of bourbon, opened it, and took a pull. When he replaced it, it clinked against a stoppered jar, and he gave a tight grin. Be a idea, he thought, to dump some of that into this booze and take another drink. One pinch, that barkeep I bought it off of said, and a man's out for eight, ten hours. Two pinches, and I expect I'd be took with the sleeping sickness 'til the whole crowd moves out. Hell, that wouldn't be square with Sam. Which also, he'd likely just have me slung over the back of some damn horse until as I woke up.

He reclosed the case and lay back on the bed. Might not be all that bad, after all, he reflected. At least Knifelips is in charge, and he's a man that knows the ins and outs of this kind of business, along with just how the Den's set up. And the other fellows, they're pretty sharp and savvy, with enough sand to see things through and not panic, even Toad and Slick Phil. Now, was that Soak and some of the others that won the cut to be in the party, I'd be a lot uneasier than what I am already, and that's plenty. All in all, the cards ran pretty good for Sam. . . .

Ten minutes later, with sleep still eluding him, he swore and sat upright. If he was going to be wakeful anyway, why waste it? Sam would be up, probably, making out lists and plans and such—might as well go get everything that he and Porky were supposed to buy all written out, and save some time in the morning.

As Faro had expected, light shone around the edges of the door to Sam Volksmacht's second-floor office. He eased it open and peered in, then stood still.

Volksmacht was seated at his desk, shuffling a deck of cards. They cascaded among his stubby fingers, seeming almost to fly of their own volition. He squared off the deck, then cut it in four places, rapidly exposing all four aces, then reshuffled and recut, laying out a royal flush.

"Sam," Faro said, stepping into the office.

Volksmacht looked up, unperturbed, and continued manipulating the cards. "Some stuff your pa taught me, years ago. Brilliant man with cards, A. B. was."

"Recollect hearing you say more'n once that you wasn't a gambler," Faro said, realizing just how it was that the group selected to attack the Tabards had been tailored to Volksmacht's specifications.

"I'm not."

Well, no. A man who could handle the deck like that, and was game to do it . . . no, not one of those cuts had been what you could call a gamble.

"Only way there was to have a chance of getting Elena back," Volksmacht said quietly. "That woman . . . well, there's no reason for me to be alive if she's not there with me. So . . . You figuring to tell people about what you just saw?"

Volksmacht's voice had been soft, but Faro sensed the intensity and desperation that underlay it. The ex-saloon keeper was willing to risk his life to go after his woman, to lay out a hell of a lot of money as well— and, it was now clear, to risk the complete ruin of his reputation. Faro wondered what he himself had ever wanted, or would ever want, that badly, and found that he could think of nothing. That kind of wanting left a man wide open to a lot of things, from disappointment to needless risk, so it was better to be without it. It would be something, just for once, though, to know what it felt like.

About everything he had ever felt in his professional life was being violated here. He had been taken for a sucker, been cheated blind, and set up to maybe get killed untimely. Well, hell, it was something new, and why not see what it would lead to?

"Tell 'em what?" Faro said. "You want to sit playing solitaire instead of drawing up battle plans and route maps and requisitions and that, it's your business. Just dropped in to ask you to make sure there's at least a couple casks of bourbon in the supplies. Death-or-glorying it is thirsty work."

Chapter 4

"We can give you ten days," Howard Barber said. "But no more, mind, Miss Garvin."

"I appreciate the generous respite," Nell said frostily. In her dealings with the business community—in this case, the political as well—she usually found it best to adopt her best grande-dame manner, dropping her natural piney-woods accent and vocabulary. And right now these fuckers has got me hoist by my twitchet on a spiny branch, she told herself, so I'd best do my grande-damnedest. "As I have told you, I have wired my partner, Mr. Blake, to return to Yuma as quickly as possible—certainly no more than ten days—in order to gain access to his assets, which will then be forthcoming to meet these . . . unexpected obligations."

Onliest thing unexpected, Nelly, is what this crowd turned out to be. Businessmen, bankers, politicians, cops, you can count on 'em to be pig-fuckers, and deal with that. But down here in Yuma, they're rat-fuckers,

44

with all kinds of new and interesting additions to the menu. Ten days ain't much, with me having no more notion than a turnip about where that Blake is or how to wire him, but it's the best I can get. Long's I can stall, I got the chance to work something out. Damn good thing that box is in Blake's name only, so's they can't get at it right off, else they'd take that and then think up something else to screw me with.

When Faro had left Yuma, Nell Garvin was savoring the triumph of her real estate and business dealings, and looking forward to adding a lot to the retirement fund she had accumulated in a San Francisco bank, maybe doubling it. But the paper partnership she had established with Faro Blake had served only to allow her to make her investments and purchases. Once it became evident that she was in fact, if not in law, operating on her own and in a fair way to become rich, the men who ran Yuma seemed to have decided that she was both defenseless and over-prosperous. Taxes on the parcels of land she owned had multiplied when the assessed valuations were raised to dizzying heights; the payoffs to the police had skyrocketed; at least three new laws the city fathers passed were clearly, and effectively, aimed at damaging her. Within a month, she was running her house at a loss, and had nearly exhausted her store of capital. Some bank loans had helped her keep going, but now they were about to be called in, just at the time when a massive tax bill was presented, with foreclosures on everything she owned as the alternative to paying.

The pattern was unmistakable. Nell Garvin, brothelkeeper from outside, had come in to Yuma and got a lock on a hell of a lot of desirable financial opportunities, and the town moguls weren't about to let her get away with it. They meant to squeeze her out and cut up what she'd got among themselves. Barber, the banker, had let her know that he'd be willing to extend her note if he could become a seventy-percent partner in her dealings, but that would have meant foregoing almost all the profits from her real estate purchases and working for what amounted to day wages in running the house. The Yuma men had pitched their demands, taxes and repayment, to well beyond what they considered she could pay, and expected her to knuckle under and sell out for the pittance she could get with them dictating who bought from her and at what price.

Ten thousand would meet the immediate calls on her and get her off the hook, but she didn't have anything like that available. Except, of course, in her retirement account. A cable to San Francisco could have the funds transferred within a day . . . but sooner than do that, she would let the whole Yuma business go down through the privy seat.

Years ago, just at the time she had switched from working for a string of madams to being one herself, Nell had decided that at forty, she would be out of the trade. She had seen too many whores and their lady managers keep at it until age, drink, dope, violence and self-disgust had made them incapable of pursuing the only occupation they knew. When she hit forty, that would be the end of Nell Garvin as a madam. And she meant to be damned sure that she would have enough to keep her as she wanted to be kept for the rest of her life. When she made her first deposit in the San Francisco bank, she swore to herself that every cent would stay there until the deadline she had set. And, no matter what temporary urgent needs had come up since then, she had kept to that oath. Once she broke it, she knew, the whole plan would be shattered; there would be another time when it would seem to be a good idea to use some of the money, just for a few months, and then another, and another . . . and there'd be another middle-aged whorehouse proprietor drifting from town to town, and getting more than middle-aged, and nothing to show for it.

Nell's suggestion of getting Faro Blake to put his ten thousand into safekeeping in Yuma had worked out more luckily than she had expected. It had been in the back of her mind for years that it would be a good thing if Faro Blake had a substantial store of cash in hand at about the time of her fortieth birthday—just maybe, with that kind of cushion, he might feel it wasn't a bad proposition to cut out of the gambling life and team up with a lady who had means of her own, such as Nell Garvin. Very far in the back of her mind, to be sure, and never consciously admitted, except during some of those wakeful moments about three in the morning, but . . .

In any case, it was encouraging that Faro had gone along with what she had proposed. And now the known presence in the Yuma bank of a large sum belonging to her supposed partner was all that was keeping her from almost immediate financial destruction.

What would happen ten days from now, that was something else. She would have to have the cash to pay out or lose everything. Well, there were two hundred and forty hours to try to think up something.

Barber interrupted Nell's reflections by saying, "I don't know that we'd be easy in our minds about your obligations to us, Miss Garvin, unless we . . . Well, there's considerable money invested and owing, and your principal creditors are entitled to see that what their funds are tied up in is operating in the way it should. Do you take my meaning?"

"I do indeed, Mr. Barber," Nell said. "You and these other gentlemen may consider yourselves privileged to examine every aspect of the operation when and as you choose."

So alongside everything else, Nell thought, they're claiming freeloading rights here, and not a damn thing I can do about it. Be something if that Blake did turn up from out of wherever in the next ten days, but that's about as likely as a cowpat teaching itself to fly. No word from him in two months, not that there ever was word from him anyway, ever since I first run across him, down there in New Mexico. Just that the trails cross from time to time, and we get together the way we get together, and then go off on our ways until the next time. Nell, you got shit for brains, you think anything's ever going to come of that.

Chapter 5

"Not much changed from what it was the last time I passed through," Knifelips Hogan said, looking through a screen of sparse, stunted trees at the slitlike entrance to Devil's Den. He was using Slick Phil Bowyer's field glasses for his surveillance—a powerful pair which Slick Phil used in a complicated racetrack scam that Faro had never got the hang of, something to do with calling the order of the horses at the far turn, then relaying the information as the basis for some last-minute side bets. As Faro understood it, this often involved Phil in hasty departures from the towns in which it was practiced.

Even without the glasses, Faro, Slick Phil, Toad Dabney, Sam Volksmacht and the others could see that Devil's Den presented a formidable exterior. A dun-colored wall of rock, striped with distorted lighter bands, extended for close to a mile either way from where they were observing, and stood a hundred sheer feet high from the rock-strewn expanse of cracked hardpan in front of it. The one break in it was a crack about four feet wide at the base, extending to little more than four times that distance at the top. The open, if broken, stretch of ground between it and the base of the hill from which they were looking extended about four hundred yards.

"Perfect killing ground," Hogan said. "Anybody comes out of there at us, we can pick them off before they get halfway. And any of us go in at them, the same applies. Old Three-Balls picked a damn good place to hole up, for sure. Just that one split, wide enough for one horse at a time, and the corrals, sheds, main house and so on 'way back in the canyon, where there's water and a little grazing."

"It is nice to know we ain't wasting our time with amateurs," Faro said sourly.

The journey from Tornup had taken just over a day and a half, about twice the time, Hogan had estimated, that Parrish Tobard would have made it in, with a presumably unwilling and bound Elena slung over the back of his horse. Now, in midafternoon, they had set up camp in a hollow on the far side of a hill overlooking the entrance to the Den. The wagon, and the tents that some of the men, with the help of Goldie and Winnie—who had, as Faro had feared, drawn the comparatively comfortable assignment of driving rather than forking horses—were setting up were effectively concealed from the sight and range of the sentries Hogan assured them were lurking in the crevice in the rockwall.

"You know the place, Hogan," Volksmacht said. "What's the best way to take it?"

"Is none, I been telling you from the start, Sam," Hogan said. "A seasoned regiment of horse soldiers might do it, given time and some heavy artillery, but, like I said, Tabard's got enough connections so that

that's not going to happen. For sure, we ain't going to
do a bit of good boiling over the crest of this hill,
ahorse or afoot, and charging 'em. There'll be two men
just inside the slit, with repeaters, unless old Three-
Balls has got softening of the brain and changed his
ways since I was here last. Even if they're only fair
shots, wouldn't about half of us get to ten yards from
the entrance. And then all of them two would have to
do is move back a few paces and pick off whoever was
coming in."

Volksmacht was wrathfully silent for a moment,
then said, "Well, hell, there's got to be something that
can be done."

"Oh, sure," Hogan said. "Don't know what good
it'll do, but it's all there is. And I best go do it now.
You, Blake, I saw you with a white hanky yesterday.
Still got it on you?"

Faro passed over the handkerchief, still reasonably
white. Hogan took it and tied it to the end of a stick.
He unbuckled his gunbelt and dropped it to the
ground.

"You going to ask for a parley?" Faro said, surprised.

"We ain't got much going for us," Hogan answered.
"We try to jump 'em, we get cut down before they
even know who we are, the way they got things set up.
I go and talk, old Three-Balls'll have a notion that Sam
is taking this serious, and it might could be that he'll
take a little longer think about things once he hears
that I'm in charge on this side. He knows me, and he
knows what I've done, and he knows that that kid of
his is a hothead that's done nothing but bring down
trouble on him. A chance he might decide to take a
strap to Parrish and turn the lady loose."

"A chance," Faro said flatly. "What kind of
chance?"

Hogan grinned and turned to Toad Dabney. "What odds would you offer, Toad?"

"Twenty to one against," Dabney said promptly.

Hogan's thin smile widened. "Man that'd offer twenty to one on that would buy gold bricks from Slick Phil, here. Hundred's more likely. But there's nothing else to go with just now."

"Hey," Faro said. "You go down there and start telling the fellows that's inside that rock there that you're here to make their boss give up something his son took, what's to say they just don't use up the loads for them repeaters you mentioned on you? My experience with folks like that, waving the white flag and not carrying your shooters don't cut enough ice to cool off a snowball in February."

"Uh-uh," Hogan said. "I was with . . . well, anyhow, I know Three-Balls, and how he handles his men. Something out of the usual comes up, they'll get to him back at the main house before they do anything. Man named Wingus, once, he thought he had a better idea about something than the boss, and did it on his own, and it turned out bad. Old Three-Balls sent him off into the badlands with his horse."

Faro thought a moment and said, "On his horse, you mean? That don't—"

"With. Tied to it and dragging behind on the ground. And the horse with a rag soaked in turpentine up its ass. I've won money on horses in races that's run slower than that, was out of sight in a few minutes, and nothing to show but hoofprints and some scrapings and stains from poor Wingus. No, Three-Balls's men don't act on their own."

"So when Three-Balls gets the word and comes up there, he'll tell them to gun you down," Faro said exasperatedly. "You being the best this crowd's got, and right to hand, he'll see the sense of that."

Hogan shook his head. "I told you, I know Tabard. Unarmed, and with your snotrag waving, I'll be okay."

He crossed the top of the ridge and pushed through the screen of trees, picking his way down the slope and across the jumble of rocks and seamed earth that lay between it and the opening into the Tabard stronghold.

"I wisht I had of thought to get him to bet on coming back alive," Faro said to Toad Dabney. "I'd of give him five-one, easy, and put up a couple hundred out of what Sam paid me. As long's he was willing to leave his stake behind, anyhow."

Knifelips Hogan's figure dwindled, but was still sharply visible in the afternoon sun as he walked toward the fissured rockwall. From the moment he had emerged into view of the sentries he had claimed were concealed in the slit, he had held his left arm well away from his side, and his right in the air, brandishing Faro's handkerchief.

When he was within a hundred feet of the slit, he stopped. The concealed watchers on the hill heard faintly: "Hold it right there! What the fuck you want?"

"To talk to Three-Balls," Hogan called.

"He ain't hirin', and he ain't buyin' encyclopedias on subscription nor parlor organs, and he has open house drawin' room receptions every other Tuesday only, so just fuck off!" came the derisive reply, underscored by a rifle shot that hit rock contemptuously wide of Hogan.

"One of you two go up to the main house and tell him it's Knifelips Hogan talking for Sam Volksmacht!"

There was a minute of silence, then a man stepped out from the cleft in the rock and leveled a rifle at Hogan. "Artie knowed you when you spoke," he called. "He's gone to fetch the old man. So you just stay there 'til he comes."

"I come all this way to see him, not figuring to go anywhere," Hogan said. He squatted on the dusty ground, rolled a cigarette, and lit it. After half an hour, he looked up at a call from behind the silent rifleman: "You, Hogan!"

On the hill, the watchers saw a movement in the entrance to the Den; then a figure emerged from its shadow. "Three-Balls, all right," muttered Volksmacht, who had commandeered Slick Phil's field glasses.

"Tabard," Hogan said, nodding. "You know why I'm here. Sam and a bunch of us are up behind the hill there, and we don't aim to cut out until we get the lady back. Sam's out for blood, but there's no sense to that. Your kid went crazy, okay, you know and I know that that's no news. You just hand her over and we'll pull stakes and forget it. Sam and her are figuring on leaving the country anyhow, so there won't be any bad feeling hanging around."

"I reamed that boy's ass when he brung her in," Tabard said. "Damn fool thing to do, no denying it."

"Well, then," Hogan said, looking a little surprised.

Tabard shook his head. "The Tabards are in the taking line, not the giving. What Parrish done'll be being talked of a good bit already, and we'd be a laughing-stock if we just turned around and gave her back. Next time we went out to work, folks just wouldn't take us serious, and we'd have to corpse quite a few to make 'em see we meant business. The money Volksmacht's got, he can buy any woman he wants, or a team of 'em. You know the setup here, Hogan. No matter how many men you got, you don't have a chance of getting in, and if you did, what was left of you would die in the slot."

"Mistake, Tabard," Hogan said.

The outlaw chief's face darkened. "Bigger one if you don't haul ass right now. You come for a parley, okay, you got it. Now, you go back to Sam Volksmacht and tell him that's all he gets. Next time I see you, you better be armed, and forget about any white flags."

Hogan sighed and rose to his feet. "Don't know what that whelp of yours wants with the lady, anyways," he said. "What one of the girls at Sam's told me, he wouldn't know what to do with her. Said he had a whang like a boiled noodle, same shape and size, and about as hard." Tabard whipped around to glare at the rifleman, who had emitted a snort of laughter, quickly stifled. "Except she could teach him knitting, or some other housewifery, so's he could be some use," Hogan continued blandly. "Maybe handling them needles would give him some ideas about how a man's supposed to be—you know, long and stiff. Well, well, give my regards to Noodle-Prod. *Hasta la vista,* Tabard." He turned and walked away.

On the hill, Faro and the others could see Hogan trudging across the open ground below the slope, with the rifleman and Tabard watching him. "This is where they backshoot him, I expect," Faro said. But Hogan continued his progress, and in a few minutes was at the top of the hill and behind the screen of trees. The two figures below vanished into the cleft in the rock.

"Well?" Volksmacht said.

Hogan shook his head.

"Damn!" Volksmacht said. "You shouldn't of risked going down. No good done at all."

"Wouldn't say that," Hogan said, and recounted the comments on Parrish Tabard that he had made to his father.

"Jesus!" Faro said. "That was putting some strain

on my hanky. What the hell'd you do that for? Surprised he didn't gun you on the spot."

"Not his way," Hogan said. "The way of it, well, no matter what old Three-Balls says about keeping quiet, that guard's going to have what I said all over the place soon's he gets off duty. Nobody much likes Parrish, and I expect he'll get some hoorawing over it. Wouldn't be surprised if somebody got the cook to serve noodles for supper tonight. Any luck, Parrish'll go wild, and there'll be some shooting. Cut down the forces a little, maybe make Three-Balls see the sense of doing like we want." He paused. "A chance of something else coming of it, too," he said. "We'll see."

The night was hot, still and oppressive. Faro, on eight-to-ten sentry duty, could hear clearly the sound of Blinky's fiddle and hoarse voice. He looked behind him at the encampment. In the glow of the dim fire around which Sam Volksmacht's army sat, he could see Goldie and Winnie, bare to the waist, doing a jig in time to the song Blinky was improvising.

"Okay," says the whore, "let's see what it's for."
Hey humpty, hey dumpty, hey jig-a-jig-jig—
But Parrish's thing was as limp as a string—
Hey randy, hey dandy, hey jig-a-jig-jig.

The girls' breasts bobbed, gleaming in the firelight as they capered to the music, hoisting their skirts high. "Be over before we get off," he muttered to Porky James, his fellow-sentry. "Anyhow, we can maybe pay a call on Winnie or Goldie during the night."

"Winnie, maybe, if she ain't tuckered out from the steady work," Porky James said. "But Hogan's let a few fellows know that Goldie's his property for the duration. Commander-in-Chief's prerogative, he says."

"Well, shit," Faro said. "Two women for twelve men, that's reasonable bivouac rations, but one amongst eleven just ain't right."

"Go argue with Hogan," Porky James said.

"Well, no," Faro said. He looked down at the moonlit rockwall that was the outer bastion of Devil's Den. Nothing was stirring there, though he was sure that their opposite numbers on the Tabard side were as wakeful and alert as he and James. He wondered what Hogan—damned woman-hog—had been hinting at with his suggestion of "something else" coming out of his confrontation with Three-Balls Tabard.

"Sing it louder, Blinky!" Hogan called from the fireside. "Let's see how far your voice can carry. Be a little entertainment for Tabard's boys down there."

Say, Parrish's prong's 'bout two inches long . . .

At midmorning on the next day, Hogan's "something else" became evident. A man pushed past the sentries at the rockwall and advanced to the middle of the open ground. The guards at the top of the hill summoned Hogan and took aim at the lone figure. "Parrish Tabard, by God," Slick Phil Bowyer said, looking through his glasses.

"No shooting yet, boys," Hogan said to the guards. He pushed through the trees and stood at the crown of the hill.

"Hogan!" Parrish Tobard yelled.

"I'm here," Knifelips Hogan called.

"You been low-rating me to my men, you cock-sucker!"

"Your daddy's men, noodle-whang!"

"God damn you, I'm going to kill you for that!"

"Come on shooting then. Expect you'll get twenty more paces, easy, before you're blown apart."

Parrish Tabard's arms sawed the air in fury. "Damn you for a coward, Hogan! You come on down here, and we'll face off fair and square, and I'll put a slug through your lying guts!"

Most of Volksmacht's party had by now drifted up to stand next to Hogan, peering at the enraged kidnapper below. "That what you was figuring on?" Faro asked.

Hogan nodded. "Parrish's thin-skinned along with being hotheaded. Bad combination. Thought there was a good chance it'd smoke him out."

"For what?" Slick Phil Boyer asked. "You go out there, and he'll have his people kill you soon's they have a clear shot, while he ducks back in."

"No," Hogan said. "You got to understand. The Tabards are a bunch of thieving, killing bastards, but there's still some rules they got to follow. See, one reason the government don't come to smoke them out is that they got connections. Lawmen, politicians and such, some as far off as Washington. They do favors for some, give some money to help elect some. It's like they've paid for a license to do the stuff they do. One of the Tabard boys has the bad luck to get arrested and in court, there's a fancy lawyer here for him, and probably a couple jurymen bought off or scared off, and maybe the judge seen to somehow. And any time there's talk of troops being called in, why, that just never gets anywheres past a certain desk in the War Department. Now, that's fine, and it's been working a while. But it'd all fall apart if it come out that the Tabards didn't keep their word. Rob, okay, kill, okay—but if they called in their guns in a fair fight that they'd set up, or shot a man that came to parley with them, then the folks they've bought or favored would figure they couldn't be trusted to hold up their end of any deals, and it's be time for the mad-dog hunt. And with Tabards knowing what they know about the folks they know about, there'd be somebody on hand to see that there wasn't a one of them left to take to jail, let alone open court.''

Hogan looked down at the waiting figure of Parrish Tabard. ''Even if that pup would dast tell the fellows behind him to shoot me, they wouldn't do it, not now that he's called for a fight.'' He cupped his hands to his mouth and called out, ''Okay, Parrish. I'm coming down. Draw when you want, I'll be ready. Get set to die with a soft-on!''

''You sure you can outdraw him?'' Faro asked as Hogan checked the cylinder of his revolver, then replaced it in his holster.

''Not certain sure,'' Hogan said, ''but pretty sure. He's about as fast as me, but he's riled, and that can cost you in a showdown. Worth the try—I get him, maybe old Three-Balls will get fed up with the whole thing. He gets me, I don't have to fret myself studying out how to get inside that damned place with enough men left to do any good.''

''Uh, good luck,'' Sam Volksmacht said.

''I hope it's better than I had on that cut of the cards with you,'' Hogan said, grinning thinly. Faro was reasonably certain that only he noticed the faint flush on Volksmacht's face.

Hogan stepped onto the slope and began his descent toward where Parrish Tabard was waiting for him. ''You want to make a bet, Phil?'' Faro said to Slick Phil Bowyer.

''Hogan or Tabard? What odds you . . . Shit, Blake, that ain't decent.''

"No, heads or tails. Heads, I get the lend of your glasses, tails, you get, oh, five dollars."

"Ten," Slick Phil said. "Got a coin?" Faro produced a cartwheel, which Slick Phil inspected carefully on both sides, after which he gave it five trial tosses. "Okay."

He tossed it, inspected the result—with Faro's alert gaze on his hand—said, "Shit," and handed over the glasses.

Faro clapped them to his eyes and watched the scene below unfold. He picked up the magnified image of Hogan, now at the bottom of the slope, and tracked him until the more distant image of Parrish Tabard came into the field of vision. The outlaw's right hand was poised above his gun, and he stood motionless, with his feet set apart and solidly on the ground. "Making Hogan come to him," Faro muttered. "Prob-'ly picked his mark, and when Hogan gets to it, he'll make his play."

As far as he could make out, allowing for the foreshortening effect of the glasses, Hogan was not much more than fifty feet from Parrish and still moving ahead.

Suddenly Hogan's left leg spraddled sideways, and he lurched violently. Both arms flailed as he tried to keep his balance. Parrish Tabard's hand dipped and darted up with his weapon, which boomed twice. Hogan was on the ground, but his revolver was out and firing. In the glasses, Faro saw three spots of red appear on Tabard's belly, chest and throat; then he disappeared from view.

Faro hastily lowered the glasses and looked at the scene directly. Parrish Tabard was down and unmoving. Knifelips Hogan was on one knee, rising to his feet. He turned and began walking back toward the hill; Faro noticed that he was limping. Behind him, two men ran out from the rockwall, scuttled to Parrish Tabard's body, and hauled it back out of sight.

In a few minutes, Knifelips Hogan was receiving the congratulations of his party. "Goddlemighty, that was a good trick," Faro said. "Let him think you're off balance, give him a chanst to draw whenas he wasn't quite set for it. But a hell of a risk. How come the gimp? He get you in the foot?"

"Both shots went over me," Hogan said. "And no, not a trick. Stepped over a rock, come down harder than I figured on, and the damn heel came off my boot."

The next question to be settled was whether Three-Balls Tabard would decide that it was time to cut his losses. "Man's got any sense," Sam Volksmacht muttered, he'll send Elena out, and there'll be an end on it, and we can all get back where we want to be."

But after an hour, with no sign of movement from the slit in the rockwall, Hogan sighed and said, "Don't look much like it. Maybe time for another parley, see what's going on."

Once again waving Faro's handkerchief, he began walking down the slope. Fire winked in the shadow of the slit, and dust fountained several yards wide of Hogan, a fraction of a second ahead of the sound of the shots. Their target was beyond effective range of anything but a sniper's rifle, but the message was clear—no more parleys.

In midafternoon it occurred to Faro that Slick Phil had never handed back the dollar he had used for the toss. He thought of seeking him out and demanding it back, but he knew that the con man would have a dozen plausible reasons for keeping it, and estimated that it would not be worth the effort. Fair enough, anyhow, to consider it as rental for the glasses. He'd seen worse shows for more than a dollar.

The mood at supper and afterwards was mixed. On the one hand, Sam Volksmacht's honor had been avenged. But that was only half the job, or maybe a tenth of it. The main thing was to get La Canasta back, and they seemed to be no further at that, in spite of a long session of earnest discussion, argument and suggestions that were usually rejected by everybody but the proposer.

"Well, now," Sam Volksmacht said finally. "Let's drop this for tonight and give ourselves a time. Blinky can make up a tune about how you done for Parrish, and the girls can dance, and—"

"Girl," Hogan said. "I got a fancy to take Goldie over to my tent and bang her 'til morning. Winnie can dance for you and whatever; Goldie's for me."

"Hey, there," Slick Phil Boyer said. "Listen, Knife-lips, you did real well today, but that don't mean you can grab off whatever you want. You kept Goldie to yourself last night, and the night we were on the trail—okay, you're the head man, after Sam—" Hogan stiffened. "—but we're got a right to pleasure ourselves, same as you. Winnie's willing, but it's asking an awful lot of a girl to keep eleven men cheered up, along with taking a hand at the cooking and so on. You wouldn't claim you had a right to a whole cask of booze to yourself, while the rest of us was getting only a cupful at a time, and it's the same thing with Goldie."

Hogan looked around the group and seemed to read their decision in the set of their faces. He turned to Volksmacht. "Your opinion on this, Sam?" he said.

"Uh . . . " Volksmacht also looked around. Faro thought he could nearly read his mind. Hogan was the linchpin of the operation and had to be catered to. But if the eleven other men turned mutinous over what they considered to be unfair treatment, they might start harboring thoughts of desertion, or at best play their parts in any fight in a lackluster way.

"The boys have a point, Hogan," he said finally. "Why don't we—"

"The boys can take their point and shove it up their asses," Hogan snarled. "Lincoln backed Grant all the way, no matter what anybody said about him. If you ain't got the sand to do that, why then, I'm resigning my commission. Find somebody else to figure out how to get into the Den without getting your balls shot off. You get some sense back in you and you want to eat some crow, you can find me in my tent."

After his departure, there was silence for a moment. "Oh, shit," Toad Dabney said after a while. "I vote we give in, let him have Goldie. He's the best we've got, and we're in deep shit without him."

Volksmacht sighed and shook his head. "No. If we do that, he's the one that's in charge, not me. If he wants to do something that's too risky, that could hurt Elena, I wouldn't be able to tell him he couldn't after that. No, I've got to appoint another head man, under me, that can lead the attack when it comes." He glowered at the ground. "But, damn it, there's still no way to get past those sentries in the slot, so no way to attack anyhow. Phil, go get out a keg of whiskey from the wagon and broach it. Maybe if we drink a little, we'll be inspired with a plan."

A moment after Slick Phil left on his errand, Faro said slowly, "I been thinking."

"About?" Sam Volksmacht said.

"How to get in. See, I think there's a way . . ."

"Could work," Porky James said, after Faro had finished his explanation.

"Should work," Toad Dabney said.

"Got to work," Sam Volksmacht said. "Yeah, we go with that."

"Well, hey," Faro said, pleased. "So now all we got to do is get someone to fill in for Knifelips when it comes to leading the running and dodging and shooting and such."

Sam Volksmacht looked at him oddly. "Settled, I'd think. You had the brains to think this up, you've got the brains to carry it out. You're the man, Blake."

Appalled, Faro watched the returned Slick Phil Boyer fill tin cups from the whiskey keg, and saw those cups raised in a toast to the party's new war chief. I come into this a foot soldier, he reflected, and here I am, pitchforked into being old Grant. Shit, just call me Ulysses S.

Chapter 6

"Hey, Ferd," one of the guards holding the entrance to Devil's Den said, "whassat?"

Ferd looked toward the ridge that led to the hill where Sam Volksmacht's invaders were encamped. Through a straggle of trees he could make out a moving shape. "Horse and rider, looks like. Maybe somebody coming with news or what for Volksmacht. Damn fool doesn't know he's about to get hisself right upside the skyline." He reached for his rifle. "Since Parrish got it, Three-Balls has said anything we can shoot up there's fair game."

Ferd waited until the horse and rider were clearly outlined against the paling sky, then squeezed off a shot. The figure seated on the horse jerked and spun away out of sight.

"Prime shooting, Ferd," the marksman's companion said admiringly.

"Better'n I thought," Ferd said. "I'd of swore I led too far, but—hey!"

The horse, bereft of its passenger, reared, screamed

and bolted off the ridge along which it had been walking.

"Coming right towards us, Ferd," the first guard said. "Lemme see can I drop him." He raised his rifle.

"What the hell for, Jake? Looks like a good enough horse. Three-Balls'll be happy to add him to the stock. Spoils of war, like."

As the runaway approached, the two guards could see that two casks were lashed to its sides behind the empty saddle. "Free supplies, too," Ferd observed. The horse slowed its run when only a hundred yards off, but continued toward where the guards were posted. Jake darted out, grabbed the reins, and hauled the animal into the entrance cleft, where it stood rolling its eyes and breathing with snorts of exhaustion and panic.

"Lessee what's in the barrels," Ferd said. "One over here's marked 'Flour.' Enough for a couple weeks' flapjacks, I'd say."

"T'other's a sight more interesting," Jake said from the other side of the horse. "Got a little spigot to it, and what's in it sloshes around some."

"What d'you suppose it is?"

"From what's wrote on it, whiskey. Guess Volksmacht's afraid of running dry up there, had it sent from Tornup. We done pretty good in the way of spoils, huh?"

"Horse, flour, whiskey, and one of those fellows done for. And all we lost so far is Parrish. I'd say we come out ahead on the exchange. You want to lead the critter back to the corral and turn the stuff over to Three-Balls, or'll I do it?"

Jake shook his head. "Three-Balls is awful strong about two guards on duty, the whole shift. Be three more hours before we're relieved—it can wait 'til then."

The two men surveyed the darkening landscape outside their post, while the horse stood quietly, its breathing subsiding to a normal rate. After a while, Jake said thoughtfully, "Three-Balls is going to be some set up about gettin' all that free booze."

"Yup."

"Accourse," Jake went on, "what's wrote on a keg ain't always what's inside of it. I mean, you could have a old whiskey keg lying around, and you could clean it out and fill it up with whatever you wanted to cart some place. Could be water, could be coal oil, anything wet."

"So it could," Ferd said. "Ain't likely, but possible."

"Now," Jake said carefully, "Three-Balls would be powerful disappointed about that. Him expecting whiskey, then when he turns the spigot and something else comes out, why, how he'd take on don't bear thinking about."

"Sure don't," Ferd said, now getting his companion's drift. "Like as not, he'd blame us for it."

"Which that wouldn't be fair, seeing's we got no way to know for ourselves what's really in it."

"By God, so we don't. Accourse . . ."

"You want to fetch over them tin cups next to the water barrel?"

Crouched below the skyline, Faro and Porky James scrambled through the scrub and trees beside the trail the horse was following, Faro guiding it with a rope loosely lashed to its bridle. "You ready with that?" he called to Porky James. "Horse'll be in sight from down there any minute."

James nodded and brandished a Y-shaped piece of wood, between the arms of which hung a length of shiny material almost an inch wide, trimmed with scallops of black lace. "Could hit a rat at thirty paces with one of these when I was a kid," he said. "A horse's ass at six feet won't be a problem. You think they'll fall for it?"

"Fair chance of it," Faro said. "The mad old Tabard's in, he'll have give orders to shoot at anything that moves up here. Just get primed, so's you c'n loose off soon's you hear the shot."

The third member of the party, slouched in the saddle, said nothing, merely swaying with the motion of his mount. Close up, the illusion of humanity was not convincing, but Faro was sure that the stuffed suit of clothes, topped by a straw-filled flour sack and broad-brimmed hat, would pass at a distance.

The last of the trees was behind them now, and horse and rider were in the open. At the distant crack of the shot, Faro, concealed by the tall grass, grabbed the dangling foot of the dummy and jerked it from the saddle, then snatched loose the horse's guide rope. At the same instant, Porky James fired his slingshot, sending a sizeable stone at the animal's flank. It reared and whinnied its protest, then, as another stone caught it in the same spot, broke away from the trail and scrambled down the incline.

Lugging the dummy, Faro and James worked their way to the next stand of scrubby trees. They stopped and peered cautiously down the hill. "Just about there," James said. "And . . . there comes one of 'em now. By God, he's taking it inside. So we brought it off."

"Maybe. We'll know that in a while. Less get back and give Toad his clothes back."

"I'll enjoy returning Winnie's garter," Porky James said, brandishing his improvised slingshot. "I better put it on her myself, just to make sure I didn't damage it any."

Faro grinned. Well, it should work, he thought. A pinch of that stuff the barkeep sold me put in a man's drink does for him, the whole batch of it in a keg ought to do the same. Now, if them two just ain't tee-total . . .

"What Hogan said before he got his feelings hurt, the guard shift'll be on 'til at least a hour after full dark," Faro said. "Plenty of time for the stuff to work if it's going to. We can head out while it's still light, though."

"But if it hasn't worked?" Sam Volksmacht said dubiously.

"Well, we'll know that soon's one of us pokes his head out in view. If they're still awake, they'll put a bullet past him."

"Or through him," Slick Phil Bowyer said thoughtfully.

Under Sam Volksmacht's direction, the members of the raiding party began checking their weapons and drawing extra ammunition. Faro walked to Hogan's tent, some distance from the others, and poked his head in. Hogan was lying on his blanket, puffing at a cigarette. "Piss off, Blake," he said.

"Just wanted to tell you you can come out in a while," Faro said, "and not have to associate with us ingrates. You and Blinky and the girls'll have the camp to yourselves."

Knifelips Hogan sat up. "How the hell's that?"

"Sam and me and the boys is paying a call on Three-Balls."

"The hell you say! You all got tired of this vale of tears and looking for a shortcut to the Promised Land?"

Faro explained his stratagem and told of its apparent initial success. "Once we're through that narrow part, it'll be dark, and we can sneak up on the house and rush it before as anyone's the wiser. 'Member, you tole us everyone'd be in the main house, that time of night, drinking and diverting or what. No guards out, 'cause Tabard's sure the sentries out front are foolproof.''

"Hot damn!" Hogan said. "That was some scheming. Could work."

"It better," Faro said carefully. "Else it'll be up to you to get the girls and Blinky back to Tornup on your ownsome.''

"Shit to that," Hogan said. "Your plan's good, but there ain't none of you got the experience to handle it. One little fuckup, and you all get shot to rags. I'll get over to Sam and the others right now, and check everything out, make sure everybody knows what he's got to do when." He stood, stooping under the low roof of the tent, and pushed out through the flaps.

"What about the Goldie business?" Faro said.

"Fuck Goldie," Hogan said, and strode toward the center of the camp.

Well, thass what the whole trouble come of, Faro said silently, as he followed.

The dusk was deepening as the raiding party walked cautiously down the slope, but there was quite enough light to pick their footing. And quite enough, Faro was painfully aware, to make them excellent targets for a pair of riflemen in the rock cleft. But Hogan's appearance on the skyline had drawn no fire, and he had signaled the others to follow him. He was fifty feet ahead of the others, and circling around to the left.

"Wants to get a straight-on look inside, I expect," Faro muttered to Toad Dabney, walking ten feet beside him.

"Also force their hand, if they're awake," Dabney replied. "Better him than me."

Knifelips Hogan made a final rush to the cleft in the rockwall, disappeared briefly, and emerged. He raised one hand to wave his party on.

One by one, the group squeezed past the motionless horse and stepped over the sprawled figures of the guards. They were breathing stertorously, and the stink of spilled whiskey rose around them. "Guess they didn't get to take more'n a couple of swallows before it hit 'em," Toad Dabney said. "Powerful stuff, all right. What's the name of the place you got it at? I want to remind myself to keep out of there, in case somebody gets careless with my drinks."

"We'll wait here fifteen minutes," Hogan said, "so's it'll be dark when we get there. Take about ten minutes to get through the narrow part here, but we'll need light to pick our footing by. You two with the lanterns, light 'em now, but be ready to douse 'em when I give the word just before we get into the open."

Faro used the wait to recheck his shotgun and verify that he was carrying a pocketful of shells. In spite of his ingrained distaste for violence, especially violence that involved him, he felt a queer excitement. It was something, after all, to have come up with a plan that had done the impossible: got intruders into the impregnable Devil's Den. Part way in, he corrected himself. I misdoubt the last couple of steps is going to be this easy.

"Lights out now—pass the word," Hogan whispered from the front of the line of men moving single-file through the narrow cleft in the massive rockbed. Metal scraped glass as the lantern chimneys were raised; then the light winked out and an odor of coal oil drifted through the passage from the smoke of the blown-out wicks. As his eyes adjusted to the darkness,

Faro could see Hogan silhouetted against the sky at the end of the passage. The stars seemed uncomfortably bright; but at least there was no moon yet.

In the open, his men gathered around Hogan. "Remember, move quiet," he said in a low voice. "Scatter just enough so's you won't bump into another man if you trip or stumble. Follow the fence here about fifty paces, then cut sharp left for a ways, and we'll be in sight of the house, far's I recall."

Faro set each foot carefully as he walked, taking pains to follow Hogan's path as closely as he could. In a few moments, a cluster of squares of light came into view around the corner of an outbuilding, and Hogan waved the party to a halt. They gathered around him. "Last stretch is open ground. No cover, but nothing likely to make you stumble. All lit up like that, them inside won't see us if they chance to look out, not until we're close enough for the light to catch us. When we're about that far, I'll give the signal, and we stop and take off our footgear. Then we rush it, moving's fast as we can without making noise." He repeated the rest of his instructions a final time, making sure every man knew his role, then moved off toward the house. Faro, as the plan called for, kept close to him.

The squares of light grew larger, and movement could be seen in the uncurtained windows. Faro heard music and voices—a rowdy ballad wretchedly accompanied on a concertina. No command performance from La Canasta, then. Good—likely enough she'd be upstairs, locked in a room, and out of the way of any gunplay; the danger to her in any fighting had been on Sam's mind. The whole business still seemed silly to Faro, but he had to admit that Sam Volksmacht's single-mindedness had brought them pretty far along in this lame-brained enterprise. And whether it made sense or not didn't matter now; what did was getting through it with a whole skin.

"Far enough," Knifelips Hogan whispered, and halted. He bent to remove his boots; the others were soon in their stocking feet. "Okay," Hogan said, and began loping toward the house.

Faro kept up with him, feeling the dry grass and occasional pebbles on the soles of his feet. The sound of music grew louder, and the words—something about a prospector who was a lot closer to his mule than he should be—clearer. The folks here didn't seem very downcast abut Parrish Tabard's death.

Then they were at the house and padding up the two steps to the front porch and across it. Men took positions alongside the front windows; Faro and Knifelips Hogan were at the front door. Three men were left in the yard to deal with any Tabard men who might be elsewhere on the premises and come at the first sign of disturbance.

"Now!" Hogan said. He kicked the door in; he and Faro charged inside; Faro, as planned, fired one barrel of his shotgun above the heads of the crowd. At the same moment, the men outside smashed the windows and thrust in the muzzles of their weapons to cover the room.

A man cleaning his revolver at a table snatched it up, then quickly dropped it as he realized it was empty. Aside from this, there was no show of resistance; without an order, the inhabitants of the large main room raised their hands. Faro supposed that the message was clear enough without words.

There were half a dozen men in the room, of whom Faro recognized only Three-Balls Tabard, and three women, none of them La Canasta. Tabard sat in a massive chair in the corner with a Bible on his lap and a pen in his raised hand; well, even outlaws keep family records, Faro thought. The concertina player's instrument hung by a strap around his neck; two men stood next to him, their mouths gaping, as if they had been caught in midnote and forgotten to close them. A man on a shabby sofa next to a used-looking woman with her skirts bunched up above her knees had removed one hand from her bodice so briskly that her breast had popped from its lodging and hung freely. The others stood or sat, frozen in the positions they had occupied when Faro and Hogan burst in.

The echo of the shotgun blast still rang in Faro's ears, and the reek of powder was strong in the air. Some of the captives' eyes turned to the jagged hole in the wall that the expanding pattern of shot had made; Faro doubted that there would be any trouble.

Toad Dabney and Porky James, careful not to get in any line of fire, moved quickly around the room, collecting weapons from those who bore them. "Not going to do a body search now," Hogan said, "but any of you that's got a sleeve gun or a sticker on you, work out how much good it's going to do you." Faro emphasized the statement by cracking the breech of his gun and putting another shell in.

Knifelips Hogan turned to the glowering Three-Balls Tabard and said, "Any more of you around?"

"You'll find out," Tabard said savagely.

"Hello the house!" came a call from outside. "What's goin' on? Me and Bill, we heard . . . aw, shit!"

In a moment, Slick Phil Bowyer ushered in two men with their hands in the air. Tabard slumped in his chair, defeat on his face; it seemed evident that the pair was the last of his forces.

"Sorry, Three-Balls," one of the men said. "Me and Bill was out at the corral, and come runnin' when we heard a shot. We thought—"

"You thought with your assholes," Tabard said dourly. "Likely you'd check if dynamite'd work by touching a match to it."

Sam Volksmacht stepped alongside Knifelips Hogan. "Where is she?" he asked harshly.

"Go fuck yourself," Tabard growled.

"They have the drop on us, Pa," a hawk-featured young woman seated alone said wearily. "No sense in playing the hand out now." She turned to Volksmacht and said, "Upstairs, room at the left at the end of the hall. The key's in the door on the outside."

Tabard swore at his daughter, then subsided into silence as Sam Volksmacht hurried from the room. He returned in a few minutes, beaming as he escorted Elena, as queenly and unruffled as ever. The impact of her presence was even more vivid than Faro remembered, and it seemed to him that maybe Sam had not been so foolish, after all. Maybe no woman was worth this kind of fuss, but if there were, she would be the one. Anyhow, we all come through it with nary a scratch, more's the wonder. Now all we got to do is get out and find our ways back, and the thing's done with—we got past the hard part, now.

Tabard seemed calmer now, and looked curiously at Hogan. "I knew you was long-headed, but it's past me how you'd have worked out a way to get in."

Knifelips Hogan jerked a thumb at Faro. "Not me, him." He explained Faro's ruse. Tabard stared at Faro with hate in his eyes. "Remember you from Yuma, a couple months back. I lost to you fair and square there, but this is different. I won't forget you, Blake."

Faro was both stung and amused at being lectured on ethics by about the most effective criminal in or near the Territory of Arizona.

Tabard's daughter glared at Faro. "That man—" She pointed at Volksmacht. "—he had some right to do this. He had a quarrel with us and he's won it. But you, and these others, you stab us in the back for money, you killed my brother for money." Her stare grew more intense as she glanced around the room. "My ma was a Gypsy," she said, "and she taught me some things. I tell you, I have the second sight, and it comes to me now that you, gambler, and those who follow you won't get out of this as easy as you think. I can see a long, terrible trip, and danger, and many of you not finishing it. And—"

Tabard was calmer now, and seemed almost amused. "Don't need any second sight for that, Cassie," he said. He turned to Knifelips Hogan. "You fellows won this round. But you ain't considered enough that you're dealing with Three-Balls Tabard. You, Volksmacht, I hear you're packed and ready to leave the country. Well, go and good riddance to you and your fancy piece. Cassie's got the right of it, you only did what you had to do. But these fellows that done it with you, why, I owe them something, so I do. I know who some of 'em are, and I can by God find out who the rest are. And you know where I got friends that pack a lot of weight, and that owe me plenty. Your bunch can't move fast enough or far enough to get away from what they can do to you. There's men that carry a star in quite a few places that'll think nothing of corpsing you, even if you ain't armed, and can rig the evidence to prove self-defense. I'm not above a half-day's fast ride from the nearest telegraph office, and once I get there, it won't be a lot of time before the word goes out on you. Yeah, I think Cassie's just about called the turn." He began to shake the chair he sat in with his laughter, and the Bible slid from his lap to the floor.

Chapter 7

He was still chuckling five minutes later, when, his hands bound behind him, he was led from the room. His adherents, similarly secured, including the women, were hustled after him. "Tie their feet up good when you get 'em to the barn," Hogan called after the last departing guard and his prisoner. "Then set 'em on the floor, far's apart as you can manage, and keep guns on every one of 'em all the time. I'll be out in a little to check."

Most of the force had left to escort Tabard and his people and see to their stowage in the barn. Only Faro, Sam Volksmacht, Knifelips Hogan, Slick Phil Bowyer and Toad Dabney remained. La Canasta sat in the corner, idly squeezing the concertina and getting a good bit more out of it than its owner had—a quiet, haunting Mexican air to which she hummed under her breath, while Volksmacht gazed dotingly at her.

"Old Three-Balls isn't just gassing, you know," Knifelips Hogan said. "He's got a lot of strings to pull, and there's no way he's not going to pull them over this business. Didn't take that into account ahead of time, though I should of." He thought a moment and gave his thin grin. "Guess I didn't figure we'd bring it off, so I didn't waste time thinking about what we'd do after. Got to give you credit for that, Blake."

"Thanks all to hell," Faro said. "Got any ideas about what comes next?"

Hogan motioned Slick Phil and Sam Volksmacht to join them. "Now Sam here and his lady, I'd say they're okay. They'll be back in Tornup soon enough and on their way, and anyhow Three-Balls said he wasn't after them, and I don't guess he'll change his mind. And whatever lawmen and politicians he's got in his pocket, there's mighty few of 'em'd care to mess with me, plus I got some connections of my own that . . . Well, I ain't worrying overmuch. But you others, that's a problem. Long before you can get to Flagstaff and onto trains out of there, Three-Balls'll be setting the wires smoking with some names and descriptions, and you will be in deep shit. If you could get a few hundred miles off, and stay away from around here until the heat dies down, you'll be safe enough, I'd say. But it's getting that far away in time that's hard to work out. No matter how we tie 'em, it'll be only a few hours before they work their ways loose, and then . . ." He shrugged.

"Easiest thing would be to shoot 'em all and burn the place," Slick Phil Bowyer said.

Hogan looked at him with distaste. "Joking," Bowyer said, though he looked wistful. "Shoot Tabard, then? A dead man doesn't have many strings to pull, I'd say."

Hogan shook his head. "When word of it got out, all of us'd be as bad off as with Three-Balls doing his worst. Murder in the first degree and accessories before and after the fact, that's what the handbills'd read, and that's what it'd be. What we get to do is get you fellows some time, and a way out of here that'll give you a chance to sidestep any shit the old man and his pals can come up with.''

'' 'S a map over there on the wall,'' Faro said. ''Looks like it might be this part of the world.''

While La Canasta played on, the men moved to the wall and studied the map. It was covered with a network of pencil marks, most of them beginning—or ending—at one point off to the right side. ''That's where we are,'' Hogan said, pointing. ''This'll be old Three-Balls's planning chart, routes to and from the jobs he pulls. Yeah, there's Tornup, and then on down there's Flagstaff. Let's see . . .''

Faro looked toward the upper left section of the map, where none of the penciled lines led. It looked like a pretty fair bet not to be Tabard territory. ''What's thisyer long, curvy line?'' he asked Hogan.

''The Colorado,'' Hogan said. ''Down there, where the line gets thicker, that's the Grand Canyon.''

''Well, hey,'' Faro said. ''That looks like a direction nobody'd be looking for us in, and we get to the river, we can just get on a boat and steam on down. Where's this thing wind up, anyways?''

Hogan looked genuinely amused for once. ''Yuma. But—''

''Well, thass fine,'' Faro said. ''I got my main grub-stake down there, and was meaning to go pay a visit to it soon. Also maybe a social call or some. And river travel's always suited me a lot better'n horseback.''

Hogan shook his head. ''Somebody went down the Colorado in a boat once, but most of them that's tried it got wrecked, drowned or both, or got their heads stove on the rocks. It ain't the Mississippi or the Missouri by a long shot, and there's for sure no steam packets making the run." He studied the map thoughtfully. "Say, that does give me an idea, though." He explained it, to Faro's growing dismay.

Hogan expounded his plan twice more, having half the guards at a time brought in from the barn. Some were dubious, others optimistic, but all admitted that it was the best chance they had to escape from Three-Balls Tabard's vengeance.

With a long stick he had found, Hogan gestured at the map. "Doesn't have to be that bad," he explained to the men. "Some rough going over the Kaibab, but in a couple of days you should be at the Colorado. Can't travel on it up here, but you can follow it down, past the Grand Canyon, then buy, rent or steal a boat down here, where it's navigable, and do the last leg into Yuma real easy. Not many towns, but there's a few, not too far from the river, where you can get supplies and maybe a roof over your heads for the night. You can take a few of Tabard's mules, and we'll give you all the supplies they can carry—we won't need hardly anything for the trip back to Tornup. A couple of pretty hard days along the way, but easier than what Tabard's got in mind for you."

He squinted again at the map. "Question is, can you get far enough off that way before Tabard gets on your trail?"

"Well, shit," Faro said. "If we got to outrun him, I as soon do it towards where there is trains and hotels and the like, 'stead of messing with rivers you can't travel on and canyons that's a mile deep, like you say the Grand is. If we can't buy some more time, I don't see the sense of it."

Toad Dabney spoke up. "I've got an idea about the time part."

"Let's have it," Knifelips Hogan said.

"I was poking around outside, took a lantern and

looked in one of the sheds. A whole lot of dynamite and blasting powder there."

Hogan nodded. "Remember Three-Balls used to make sure of having some on hand. Handy to blow a safe with, or block a road so's a stage'd have to stop right where he wanted it."

"Well, that's it, d'you see?" Dabney said eagerly. "We hump that stuff out to the front end of that passage, and we put it where it'll do the most good, and touch it off. Be a couple tons of rock blocking it. Even with all Tabard's men coolieing it, it'd be another day or so before they could get out and get on with what he's got in mind."

Hogan brightened. "Damn good idea. We'll set one charge halfway down the passage, another at the end. Maybe it'll only make a couple of damn big piles, that a man could climb over in a pinch, but there's no way to get a horse through there unless it's most cleared away."

"Hey," Slick Phil Bowyer said. "How about we shoot all the horses? Then they won't follow us at all."

Hogan gave him a disgusted look. "That'd be about two degrees short of the hot water you'd be in for shooting the whole bunch of them, women and all. And I'd not be a party to it, I'll tell you."

It seemed to Faro that Knifelips Hogan liked horses better than he liked most people. Maybe he'd been hanging around with the wrong crowd.

"Now," Hogan went on, "like I said, I'm cutting out with Sam and Elena, get back to Tornup with them and Blinky and Goldie and Winnie, and fend for myself after. So you fellows got to have a leader to keep things together and see to fair shares of supplies and so on, like a patrol commander or a wagon train captain, d'you see?"

Why's Toad looking at me that way? Faro wondered. And Porky? And Slick Phil? And . . . Oh, shit. Shit, shit, and shitfire. What was Abe Lincoln's story about the fellow being ridden out of town on a rail? "If it wasn't for the distinction of it, I'd decline the privilege," 's what he said. Hell, though, Blake, look at it this way: you want Porky James or Toad Dabney or such leading you through the valley of the shadow of death, or wherever the hell this tour's taking us?

Five minutes later, the matter was settled by acclamation, the brief delay caused by the necessity of sending a man to the barn to explain the proposed election of a leader and the one candidate for the job to the guard contingent there and return with their verdict, which was unanimous.

Knifelips Hogan pulled out the tintacks that held the map to the wall, folded it and handed it to Faro. "You'll be needing this to navigate," he said.

"That, six rabbits' feet, two horseshoes, a half-pint of four-leaf clovers, and a medicine man's spirit bag," Faro said sourly around the cheroot he was smoking.

Hogan clapped him on the back. "Good you can joke about it. Things get rough, a sense of humor can see a man through."

Faro's teeth met through the butt of the cheroot, which scattered sparks as it hit the floor.

At first light, Hogan roused the half of the party sleeping in the main house, ordered breakfast prepared from Tabard's stores, and set about gathering the explosives. These were loaded onto mules which were then led to the narrow passage to the outside world. Faro was one of those accompanying them. The two Tabard guards who had been left by the exit giving onto the stronghold were awake now and whimpering as they struggled against their bonds. Hogan ordered their removal to the barn, and that they be given water if they wanted it.

"Jake and me, I don't think we're never going to drink anything else ever again," one said huskily. "If whiskey ain't safe, what is? You want to do me a favor, ast somebody to pull that railroad spike out of the top of my head."

In daylight, the trip through the passage was easier and quicker than the first one had been, even with the mules along. "First charge here, I'd say," Hogan announced, pausing where there was a sizeable amount of rubble in the path. "Lots of loose rock ready to come down, and that hell of a big overhang up there. Leave off two casks of powder and a dozen sticks of dynamite, then let's get on out front."

At the entrance to the Den, the decoy horse still stood patiently, staring at them glassy-eyed with its front legs spread at a strange angle. "Shit," Hogan said, "the poor critter must've licked up some of the whiskey that was still in the cups. Oh, hell."

Hogan patted the animal on the nose. "You'll be okay, boy," he said soothingly. "You're a big old horse, horse, and you can take a little doctored booze and just piss it away, soon's you're up to it. Here, you, Blake, knock the top out of that water barrel and bring it over to him."

Faro pounded in the top of the cask with the butt of his gun, and hauled it to the horse, which drank thirstily. "Lessee," he said to Hogan. "You went up against Parrish Tabard, shot him dead, then you took over the raid and pushed into old Three-Balls's place, which that could have got all our asses, including yours, shot off, and then you got a whole bunch of people tied up and laid out in that barn, and never turned a hair through the whole of it, far's I seen. And now you're all tremblesome and concerned over this crowbait."

"Well, hell," Hogan said. "I mean, horses, they're not the same thing as people. You can trust a horse, the way you can't trust a person. You give a horse something, you know what you're going to get out of him."

True enough, Faro thought. Give him hay, get horse-shit.

While Hogan superintended the placing of the charges at the entrance, Faro walked up the hill to the encampment and greeted Winnie, Goldie and Blinky Castle, who had bacon frying and coffee just off the boil.

"When there wasn't any shooting when you all went in," Goldie said, "we figured it was going okay. We had our fingers crossed all night that it was working out for you in there. Guess it must've, or you wouldn't be here. Anybody hurt?"

Faro sipped at the hot brew and shook his head. "No bloodshed, and only one shot fired." He recounted the events of the last twelve hours, to the girls' appreciative murmurs and Blinky's avid interest.

"Glory be!" the old singer and fiddler said. "I'd of given a pretty to see that! 'Course, I'd give a pretty to see anything, come to that." He cackled briefly and said, "Blind joke, I make 'em now and then so folks'll feel easy around me, they don't have to worry about old Blinky's feelings."

"Old Blinky was feeling pretty good last night," Winnie said tartly. "Me'n Goldie, we kept our fingers crossed, like she said, but old Blinky worked it out so's our legs damn sure wasn't. He was at us both, one at a time and together, in a way you wouldn't believe.

"Like I always say," Blinky said proudly, "a man

loses one power, Providence sees to it that the others get some kind of increase to make up for it."

"If I ever learn you've gone deaf," Goldie said, "I'll take steerage passage to about anywhere. I don't believe I could stand any increase in the power you was working on last night."

"An artist has to live flat out," Blinky said. He cocked his head toward Faro, his filmed eyes apparently looking keenly just past Faro's left shoulder. "Now, that is some tale you just told," he said. "I am going to turn it into one humdinger of a song, the whole business, right from where that Parrish started it, to where you sneaked into Three-Balls's hideout and took over. If I do it right, folks'll be singing it for a lot longer than I'm around."

"There'll be another one you can do, anybody gets through to tell about it," Faro said. He outlined the unforeseen problem that Three-Balls Tabard had presented them with, and the proposed solution of a perilous trip down, or alongside, the Colorado River. The old man crowed gleefully. "Just one survivor, that's all I need, to let me know what happened! You tell those fellows, if any of 'em make it, to look me up and gimme the whole tale. Two songs like that to my name, I don't expect anybody'll ever forget old Blinky!"

As Faro picked his way down the hill, he heard the blind fiddler beginning to confect a lyric drawn from the events of the last day.

> *Now, Blake was the man that come up with the*
> *notion*
> *To send in the whiskey upon a white horse.*

Piebald, Faro thought. Do poets lie because they like to, or because they're too lazy to get it right?

He poured in a kind of a devilish potion
That hit those poor buggers with terrible force.

"Anybody left anything behind in there?" Knifelips
Hogan called. "Once we blow this, there's no going
back."

When there was no reply, he waved the rest of the
party on ahead, and touched a match to the long fuses
that had been fixed to the first charge of dynamite and
powder halfway down the twisting corridor that led
from Three-Balls Tabard's fastness.

They moved briskly and were in the open when the
ground shook with the explosion. Some loosely em-
bedded rock in the outside wall crashed to the ground.
Five minutes later, Faro, Hogan and Sam Volksmacht
walked cautiously down the passage and surveyed the
mound of shattered stone that rose almost thirty feet
above the path. "About how I figured," Hogan said.
"Okay, let's get out and do the next one."

The second and last demolition worked even more
effectively than the first. To the accompaniment of
multiple bangs, as the dynamite exploded the blasting
powder, slabs of rock toppled through blooming
clouds of smoke and came to rest in a giant jumble,
masking what had been the only entry to Devil's Den.

It was not much past noon when Faro, at the front of
those who had chosen him to lead them, sat on his
horse and watched the departure of the six who, safe
from Three-Balls Tabard's vengeance, were bound for
Tornup. Sam Volksmacht and Knifelips Hogan rode on
either side of the wagon; Goldie, Winnie, Elena and
Blinky Castle rode in it, with Goldie at the mules'
reins. Blinky was facing backwards, sawing at his
fiddle. Just before the track turned and took them out
of sight, the three women turned and waved.

"She's something, that there Elena," Porky James sighed.

"All women are something," Faro said. "Thing is to keep in mind what." He looked behind him and surveyed his followers: twelve mounted men and three mules piled high with casks, sacks, cases, blanket rolls and tied-up tents. He raised his right hand high, and made a chopping gesture toward where he fervently hoped the Colorado River lay.

"We got a distance to go, you men!" he called. "Less move the hell out!"

Chapter 8

"Where the hell are we?" Faro asked morosely.

"Why the hell are we?" Toad Dabney said, in about the same spirit. "How the hell we are, I know, and it's not good. Lemme see what I can make out from the map." He unfolded the large square of paper that Knifelips Hogan had taken from Three-Balls Tabard's wall and which Faro had entrusted to his safekeeping. "Somewheres in the coconuts, it looks like." Faro drew his horse closer to Dabney's and grabbed at the map.

"Coconino Plateau," he said after a moment's study. "If that dry creek we passed over this morning's the same thing as this bitty line on the map, anyhow. There ain't nothing about coconuts into it."

"I misread it," Dabney said. "Sweat was running into my eyes so's I couldn't read right."

"Well, we ain't that far from the river," Faro said. "We get to the river, we'll be okay."

"I won't be okay 'til I have my heel snugged up against a bar rail, in a place that has the blinds drawn against the heat of the day, and a sympathetic soul filling up a tall glass with shaved ice and bourbon and topping it with some crushed mint and shoving it across the mahogany at me," Dabney said. "Then's when you're talking about okay, not getting to some place that's even more godforsaken than this, most likely. Hey, Blake, we going to live on this same stuff much longer?"

The first half-day's progress away from Devil's Den had been easier and more manageable than Faro had expected. The men had accepted his leadership, and the route had seemed easy enough to follow. At the halt that night, there had been enough food—based mostly on dried apples, slab bacon, and rice, but Porky James, who made a habit of cookery, had put the ingredients together with some spices and come up with something fairly palatable—and enough drink to make the voyagers content and prepare them for a good night's sleep.

The next day had produced a good breakfast—an apple dish flavored with bacon—which had helped dispel the hangovers the bourbon included in the supplies had induced in all except Porky James and a man called Jarvis, who had stuck to coffee. Faro remembered them as nondrinkers from Sam Volksmacht's party, and asked them how it was that they were declining one of the few substances that made horseback travel, and the arid country they were traversing, bearable.

"My stummick," Porky James said, patting the convexity that lapped over his belt buckle. "Tore all to hell inside, the docs tell me, and gripes me like I couldn't tell you. No booze for years, if ever, they say, and a snort or so and I'm a dead man."

"Mine is a sad story," Jarvis said mournfully. "As a lad, I—"

"Works out to something lousy happened, and you're off the sauce for good, that it?" Faro said hastily.

"Ah, yes," Jarvis said.

"I'll take the rest as read," Faro said. Command was a habit new to him, but he was beginning to learn that it had its prerogatives, one of which was being able to cut off conversations that looked like being tedious.

The second night's supper was a good deal less successful than the first, though essentially the same, which was the problem. "Well," Porky James said, when the monotony was protested, "I have to make do with what there is. Dried apples, bacon, rice, they travel well and don't spoil fast, but they don't make for anything much in the way of fancy eating. There's some canned tomatoes I was saving for a treat for Sunday, but I can put them in with the bacon tomorrow night if you want." The promised delight had not done much for the group's mood, and the liquor supply had received a substantial assault.

Now, riding alongside Toad Dabney, Faro was aware that the hard journey through the broken country, especially with a varying range of hangovers, was taking its toll of his men's morale. "I should of taken more time before we started," he said, "and butchered a calf on Tabard's place for fresh meat to bring along. It'd of held for a few days anyhow, even in this heat, and it'd of made a difference to the eating."

"Sure would have," Dabney said. "But you didn't, did you?"

Another aspect of command was having to live with what you might have done, but hadn't. Faro consulted the map again. "If we're about where I'd guess we are," he said to Toad Dabney, "there's a town somewheres around here, Herriman. Off our route some, but if we knowed just where it was, we could send a couple of fellows in for some fresh meat and other stuff. Needn't cost us too much time, 'cause they could ride pretty fast, not have to keep back to the pack mules' pace."

"Fine," Dabney said. "But that doesn't do us much good if they don't know how to get there, does it? That'd be a nice job, though—a chance there's a saloon, if there's a town, and it'd do me a power of good to pay a visit to such. There's plenty of booze with us, but it ain't the same thing swigging it warm out of a tin cup in the open as it is to lean on a bar or sit down and have it poured over a couple big chunks of ice."

Faro instantly decided the composition of his purchasing commission, should it become possible to send one out: Porky James and Jarvis. Dabney or any of the others would almost certainly put in some saloon time, and get back to the camp dangerously late, if ever. There was also the chance that, in their cups, they would blab about their recent adventures. And, if Three-Balls Tabard had eyes and ears in the place, that could put him on their trail a lot sooner than would be comfortable. The only prudent course was to send the nondrinkers. He was pleased with himself; that was the kind of thinking Ulysses S. would have come up with. Now the only thing was to find out how far away this Herriman place was and how to get to it.

A rare stream and a straggle of trees showed up ahead on the dusty track at just about the right time for the noon halt. When Faro drew his men up at a likely spot, he found it occupied.

"*Hola, señores,*" one of the two men seated in the shade of a tree said cheerfully. He was small, sharp-faced, big-nosed, with a wispy, stiff moustache, and most of his features shaded by a sombrero. His companion was larger and moon-faced, with an amiably simple expression, and was strumming a guitar and singing off-key. As far as Faro could tell, the song had a good chance of being "Mariquita Linda." Two capable-looking cow ponies were tethered to trees a little distance away from them.

As the new arrivals dismounted, the small man said, "I am Ignacio and this is my partner, everybody calls him Gato Loco, he's a little, you know?" He whirled an index finger next to his temple. "But a nice *hombre*, no harm in him."

While Porky James sweltered over a brushwood fire to produce biscuits to accompany the cold canned beans for lunch, Faro talked with Ignacio and found that he and his companion were casual laborers— cowboys, handymen, bricklayers, whatever there was a demand for that did not call for overmuch training. More importantly, they were bound for Herriman. "Gato and me, we just got paid off at the last place, now we like to have some fun. Herriman not much of a place, but there's saloons where a man can enjoy— other things. When Gato playing his guitar in saloons, people give him much money so he'll go play somewheres else."

Faro learned that Herriman was about three hours' ride at a brisk pace to the southeast, along a clearly marked track, and that Ignacio and Gato Loco would be glad of company along the way.

He drew Jarvis and Porky James aside and said, "Now, that's the straight stuff about you fellows not going for the booze, ain't it?" When he had received their assurances, he outlined their mission. Porky James was cheered at the prospect of being able to secure such delicacies as fresh beef and eggs.

There was a near-mutiny among the rest of the party

when Faro announced his intentions. "Well, hey," Slick Phil Bowyer said, "whyn't we all going? Put up some place there for the night, have ourselves a time, that'd be the ticket."

"Horses go faster than mules for one," Faro said. "Riding time and buying time for Jarvis and James, that's seven, eight hours. With our pack mules, maybe treble that, a whole day, and no saying what Tabard's up to by now. And two men can get into a place and out, and not much notice taken. The whole bunch of us show up, and anybody Tabard might of got to is bound to know just who we are. We'll just rest up here and send Porky and Jarvis out, and wait for 'em to come back with the fixings for a damn fine supper. Maybe a little late, since it'll be about nine before they get back, but worth waiting for."

Faro's argument eventually mollified the men, and they settled in to lounge in the shade of the trees as Jarvis, Porky James, Ignacio and his friend rode off to the southeast.

"Any minute now," Slick Phil Bowyer said, looking at his watch. "They left at half after noon, and it's just on eight."

"Steak," Toad Dabney said dreamily. "Steak, and fried onions on the side . . . You did tell 'em to get onions, didn't you, Blake?" At Faro's nod, he went on, "We best get a fire going. Soon's they show up, I want to have those steaks a-sizzling and a-dripping fat and smelling so fine. . . ."

"Just as well they didn't get here before now," Toad Dabney said with forced cheerfulness. "Takes a while for a fire to burn down to the coals, the way it is now, but that's the only way to cook steak. When the wood's still flaming, you get the meat all smoky and sooty." He looked to the southeast through the dimness of late dusk.

"A thing I always wondered," Slick Phil Bowyer said, working a can opener around the top of a can of stewed tomatoes. "They started canning stuff about eighteen and twelve, but they didn't invent the can opener until about fifty years after. How the hell did they get at the food until then?"

"Ghosts," Toad Dabney said, setting an opened can down on the faintly smoldering coals. He gulped at the whiskey in the tin cup he had set on the ground next to him.

"What's ghosts got to do with it?

"Goats, I mean. See, goats eat kin tans, I mean tin cans, see, so they must've given the can tins to a goat or so and had it eat off the top, then they could scoop out what it was that'd been tin-canned."

"I didn't know that," Slick Phil said, taking a long drink from his own tin cup.

"Nor I didn't, but it sounds right, don't it?"

Slick Phil thought for a moment, then shook his head. "No, it doesn't. How'd anyone know in the firsplace that a goat'd eat tin cans before there were tin cans? You just don't make a tin can and then say, 'Hey, maybe a goat'll want to eat on this—commere goaty, I got something for you.' There's steam coming up from the cans here, let's dish this shit out."

As Bowyer and Dabney slopped the warmed tomatoes onto plates and handed them up unsteadily to their hungry and by now drunken comrades, Faro looked for the hundredth time in the direction that

Jarvis and Porky James had taken—almost twelve hours ago.

Morning brought sun stabbing into Faro's eyes, awakening him to a pounding headache and a mouth that felt like a cougar's armpit. It might have been a mistake to keep up with the men in their drinking last night—first in anticipation of a prime feast, then to console themselves for its absence—but then, Ulysses S. Grant hadn't been noted for his abstemiousness, either. Maybe a general thought better with a hangover.

He wrestled out of his blanket and lurched over to the cookfire. Toad Dabney had just succeeded in scorching half a pan of bacon, leaving the other half raw. "Can't seem to get the hang of it," he said.

Faro shuddered at the smell of burned meat, and said, "Don't think you'll have many customers this morning for anything but coffee."

Dabney shook his head. "The thing you want after a hard night's drinking's food. I've been so bad my eyelashes hurt, but once I got around a couple of fat pork chops, some fried potatoes and onions, and—"

"I want a fucking menu, I'll go to a restaurant," Faro said, just managing to keep from gagging. "Lemme at that coffee."

It was not good coffee, but it was coffee, and it did its work. After half a cup, his innards felt a good deal steadier, and the tracklaying team in his head took a rest break. He looked around the camp. Three men were up, one sitting against a tree, the others walking dazedly. Some of those still in their blankets were stirring feebly and plucking at the ground; others lay like logs, mercifully unaware of what awaited them when consciousness returned. Faro promised himself that any man who woke up in good spirits and unimpaired vigor would draw the dirtiest detail he could think up.

Two unused blanket rolls testified to the continued absence of Porky James and Jarvis. Toad Dabney gave up his efforts at the cookfire and joined Faro, gnawing a chunk of red-white-and-black bacon. "They didn't come back," he observed.

"Not 'less they're roosting in a tree like buzzards," Faro said.

"What d'you expect happened to them? Somebody in Tabard's pocket spotted 'em? Those two Mexes robbed and corpsed 'em for what they had?"

Faro shook his head—a major mistake, but a little short of fatal—and said, "That runt, not much bigger'n a mouse, and the loon with the guitar? Doubt it. Jarvis and Porky is armed, and they been around. The Tabard business, I don't think so neither. Hardly been time for him to get on the wires, and those two ain't among the men he knows by name." He set down his cup and headed for his horse. "I best go see for myself," he said. "You keep a eye on things for me, Toad, whiles I'm gone. If I ain't back by late afternoon, figure there's trouble of some kind and make sure to put out guards. If I ain't back by morning, you can be damn sure there's trouble, and you'd better all move on, best's you can. The map's in my gear."

The general hands over to trusted second-in-command, Faro thought, as he rode down the track Ignacio had claimed led to Herriman. First Faro Blake in charge of that crew, then Toad Dabney. What a bunch of out-of-luck fuckers.

He reached Herriman in late morning. It was a sunbaked town with a few trees, larger than he would have expected from his journey through this desolate area, and gratifyingly provided with saloons, along with other mercantile establishments. He dismounted and tethered his horse outside the butcher shop, and entered it.

The butcher disclaimed all knowledge of a fat man and a tall, thin one dickering for prime beef the day before or at all recently. Nor had the grocer dealt with any such, or the keeper of the general store.

So maybe they was funning me about not being drinkers after all, Faro thought. Best try the saloons.

Inquiries at the nonalcoholic merchants had not required purchase, but saloon etiquette was different. Besides, it had been a hot, dusty ride, and on an empty stomach. The first place he tried was, to his pleased surprise, able to produce an egg to be beaten up in a glass of brandy. Once his breakfast was down, and seemed likely to stay in place, he asked about Jarvis and Porky James, without result.

The second, third and fourth of Herriman's saloons were equally unproductive of information, but after his visits to them, Faro felt a good deal more alert and robust.

"*Señor,* is good to see you." Faro blinked and saw the diminutive Ignacio standing on the plankwalk in front of him. Gato Loco grinned foolishly over his companion's shoulder.

"Hey, what happened to my friends?" Faro said. "Them two you rode in with?"

Ignacio shrugged. "I show them where is the places that sell what they want to buy, then Gato and me, we go on to the saloons, I don't see them after."

Gato seemed to be following the conversation, and grinned. He tugged at the loose collar of his shirt and said, *"Camisa."*

"Oh, yes," Ignacio said. "Funny thing, we pass laundry, about edge of town, fat man, he sniff air like horse, he say to other man, 'Maybe we better get our shirts wash and iron while we here,' and other man say that damn good idea. Seems to me, you going to be on trail many days, who needs clean shirt?"

"Huh," Faro said. "You fellows mind taking a little walk with me, show me this laundry place?"

"A pleasure, *señor*."

Standing with the two other men outside Wu Fan's Laundry, Faro could see nothing strange about it, nor any reason why Jarvis and Porky James should have been seized with a passion for fresh haberdashery. He sniffed the air and caught the standard laundry smell of starch and steam. Then he stiffened. There was another, subtler, sweet element to the aroma.

He moved around to the alley alongside the laundry. Gato Loco and Ignacio followed curiously. The rear of the laundry was a good bit larger than the business seemed to call for, and there was a back entrance. Faro sniffed again. No starch and steam here, but a stronger whiff of the pungent scent he had detected from the main street. Herriman might be a one-horse burg, but it had evidently acquired some big-city refinements. A big city like San Francisco, for instance.

He stepped to the door and knocked on it. It opened a crack and a Chinese face peered out. *"Yen shee gow,"* Faro said.

"One pipe, two dolla, two pipe for three dolla, good boggin," the face said.

Faro slammed the door open, drawing a squawk of protest from its keeper, and strode into the room, still followed by Ignacio and Gato Loco. The air in the room was hazy with the fumes of opium. Four patrons lay on cots, holding long pipes from which aromatic smoke drifted. Two of these were Jarvis and Porky James, only vaguely conscious.

"You not bust in here!" the proprietor scolded. "I

pay cops, everything! You get out, else you in trouble."

"Be out soon enough," Faro said grimly. "Just collecting my friends here."

He went over and stood between the cots where James and Jarvis lay. "Fine brace of men I picked for a important job," he said bitterly. "The only two in the crowd that don't drink, I figured, so they'd be safest to send."

Porky James grinned at him loosely. "Hey, Blake," he mumbled. "We told you true, we're blue-ribbon, teetotal and all that. But you never ast us if we was hopheads."

Chapter 9

The opium-den proprietor was shrilling furiously at Faro, tugging at his sleeve. "Cool down," he said. "Don't mean to disturb your trade, but I got to get these fellows back where they belong."

"I call cops!"

Faro glanced at Porky James, who had been carrying the funds for the shopping trip in a wallet in the side pocket of his trousers. The pocket fabric was sticking halfway out of the opening. Could do some cop-calling myself, but I expect this fellow's got his arrangements with the local law. . . .

"You Wu Fan?" he said.

"Yes! Respect'ble local merchant! Now, you—"

"Tsai Wang told me to give you his regards, was I ever hereabouts," Faro said, staring hard at the man.

Wu Fan's bluster evaporated instantly. "Tsai Wang from San F'cisco?"

Faro nodded. "Tsai Wang and me go back a long ways. He's a, uh, righteous man under heaven, old

Tsai Wang is." Tsai Wang, as a matter of fact, was San Francisco's major fence, drug importer and purveyor of any illicit service, from whoring to murder, but the roughly translated Chinese phrase conveyed his implacable intention to stand by his friends and see that his enemies did not prosper. "You ever eat in that private room of his?" Faro went on. "I tell you, digging into them thousand-year eggs, while as you're looking at all that jade carving and them screens, why, that's something to remember."

Wu Fan gulped. "Not had chance to visit honorable Tsai Wang for long time." Never, you backwoods piker, Faro thought. But you sure as hell know about him.

"Well, he'll be glad to hear you're doing good business out here," Faro said genially. "Say, what do I owe you for what my friends smoked?"

"Ah . . . they pay first, nothing to pay now," Wu Fan said huskily.

"Well, I am glad to see you took such good care of them. It ain't my diversion, but if they got to do it, I'm happy to see that they come to a place where the customers or what wouldn't take advantage of 'em while they're nodding off. Old Tsai Wang, he's always saying that it don't matter what kind of place you're running or what you're selling, so long's the customer's safe and gets fair value for his money."

"Ah . . . right," Wu Fan said. "I take good care my clients. They have money, watches, things that cost much, I keep safe in my office 'til they ready to go. Your friend, he have wallet, some money, I don't want him to lose it, so I . . . I go get now."

While Wu Fan darted off on his errand, Faro, with the aid of Gato Loco and Ignacio, got Jarvis and Porky James to their feet and marched them toward the door. Outside, Faro took a deep breath and shook his head.

The opium fumes in the room had made his head buzz slightly, and he felt strangely at peace with the world and disinclined to give his errant subordinates the reaming they deserved. That is dangerous shit, all right, he thought, when it don't let a man even keep a good mad on.

Wu Fan appeared at the door and thrust Porky James's wallet at Faro. "You friend money," he said. "Next time you in San F'cisco, you please tell honorable Tsai Wang Wu Fan run good place, yes?"

"For sure," Faro said. After the door had closed, he counted the money in the wallet. He had sent Porky James off with a hundred dollars, more than enough to cover the most exorbitant charges for provisions. There was now two hundred in it.

Evidently Tsai Wang's name carried a lot of weight—and evidently Wu Fan was a firm believer in insurance premiums.

Porky James and Jarvis were still rubber-legged and over-happy, but Gato Loco and Ignacio jumped at the chance to earn ten dollars to help Faro shop and load his purchases on his horse and James's and Jarvis's, which he had found hitched to a rail on a side street. They were at least in good enough condition to be hoisted into their saddles and stay there as their mounts plodded out of town. There was a final burst of song and strumming from Gato Loco as they departed—"Mariquita Linda" again.

The three-hour ride was enough to bring Porky James and Jarvis back from whatever happy land they had been touring. "Listen," Porky said, shamefaced, "it was just that after the fight at Tabard's, you other fellows, you had ways of unwinding, the booze and all. Jarvis and me, we didn't have that, so when we got a snuff of that stuff going past the laundry, why, we just naturally had to look in and see if our noses had gotten it right. And there it was, and we . . ."

"Fucked up," Faro said. "There's a day lost, and God knows what the rest of the boys have been up to while I been gone. Was I them, I'd lynch you on general principles."

But to keep the peace, he contrived an account of the two men's discovery of a bare butcher shop, with new meat promised for the next day, as an excuse for the delay.

"Where'd you sleep?" Slick Phil Bowyer asked enviously. "A hotel, clean sheets and a thundermug right handy by the bed?"

"Local businessman let 'em have the use of a couple of cots in a back room he wasn't using for anything else," Faro said. Part of the art of command was knowing when there was just no damned use in punishment.

Any further questions the members of the band who had remained at the encampment might have had were waived as the scent of the steaks and sweet corn Porky James was broiling filled the grove.

"Shame you and Jarvis don't drink," Dutch Schroeder called to Porky James. "Meal like this, *ganz gut,* it's the better for the bite of some whiskey with it."

"Jarvis and me, we don't need the booze to enjoy ourselves," Porky James said blandly.

"Well, that's it."

"That for sure is it."

"Big fucker, ain't it?"

"There it is, all right."

The travelers sat their horses and surveyed the incomparable vista of the Grand Canyon of the Colo-

rado, stretching an unfathomable distance across and
what looked like a mile down, its flanks and escarp-
ments sculptured in strange shapes, striped with alter-
nating layers that glowed in the late-morning sun, a
stone manuscript of hundreds of millions of years of
rise and fall, of life and death, and paid tribute to it
with what eloquence they possessed.

Faro squinted down and saw a thread of silver far
below—the Colorado itself. No, it wasn't any kind of
river where you'd expect the *Robert E. Lee* to come
steaming along and tie up at the levee.

Toad Dabney edged his horse close to the edge of
the precipice and looked over. "I have spat eight feet
into a cuspidor in the Butler House Hotel," he said,
"and never stained the sides. That is some spitting.
But now, I can by God spit a whole damned mile!" He
did so.

The lie of the land obliged them to angle away from
the edge of the Canyon as they moved south. The area
was mostly rock and dried earth, but there was an
occasional fertile valley, with sparse grass on the hills
above it. In one of these they found some wandering
sheep and a sheepherder, tending his flock on horseback.

Faro hailed him. "Know of a place we can stay
around here? Stand of trees, maybe a stream next to
it? Feels like a over-cool night coming on, and we ain't
got but blankets to shelter with, so some cover'd be
welcome."

The sheepherder approached, and Faro saw that he
had only one working eye; the other was a seamed
pocket of flesh. "Don't need to study out trees," he
said. "Big old stone barn a little ways along, weather-
tight. It's on my grazing land, but I don't mind letting
folks that's passing through peaceable have the use of
it for a night."

He spoke with a slight accent, and Faro suspected that, like most sheepherders out here, he was a transplanted Basque. The name he gave, Rep Sandoz, pretty much confirmed that impression. He accepted Sandoz's offer with gratitude, and in a reasonable time before sunset, they were established by the building, with Porky James preparing dinner, small pieces of choice steak baked in pastry in an improvised oven.

Faro shivered briefly as he ate; the weather was changing, and the evening winds were cooler and keener than any they had experienced on the trail so far. When he had eaten, he rose and took Toad Dabney and Slick Phil Bowyer with him to inspect the barn. It was spacious, about eighty by forty feet, with twenty-foot-high walls of stone that appeared to be at least two feet thick. A massive wooden door hung open on iron hinges. The floor was smooth packed earth, with a scattering of straw.

"Snug enough for the night," Faro said. "Whoever built it knowed what he was doing. You keep critters in here against the storms or what, they ain't going to get out 'til you're ready to let 'em."

There was some drinking and talking around the cookfire after the meal had ended, but the chill of the evening and the fatigue of the day's travel cut it short. By nine, Faro and his men were rolled in their blankets on the floor of the barn. He had debated leaving a sentry outside to watch over the horses, mules and supplies, but decided against it. It would be damned uncomfortable duty, demanding cutting down on the sleep of two men, given two shifts, and there was scarcely any menace to be expected in this place, desolate of anything but sheep. He had the barn door propped open so that any disturbance, however unlikely, would be known to them.

He slept deeply, but it seemed to him that, in the vague dreams that drifted through his mind, there was an eerie screeching, like the cry of a vengeful ghost.

When Faro awoke he thought it was still the middle of the night. It was completely dark, yet he had the feeling of having slept about as much as he always did. He struck a match and consulted his watch: six-thirty. The sun should have been up long since. He rose to his feet, struck another match, and, by its flickering light, picked his way among the blanketed sleepers to the doorway that should have framed the morning sky.

On the contrary, it was filled with the heavy beams of wood that comprised the door he had left ajar the night before. He shoved at it and was unable to achieve the least budge. Barred from the outside, then. That would be the screech he'd registered in his dreams, the protest of the hinges moving under the weight of the door. Take the business a step further, it had been barred by someone. Who? And why?

Half an hour later, both questions were answered. A tattoo on the door, that sounded as if an axe helve were being pounded on it, was followed by a call. "Anybody awake in there?"

Faro sensed a stirring behind him, and said, "One now, the rest in a bit. What the hell's going on? And who's that?"

"Your friend Rep, your host. You're such good guests, I'm going to keep you a while. You get tired of my hospitality, in there in the dark, no food, no water, no light but what you got with you, that's a shame. Because you're going to be there the rest of your lives. You won't starve, you got each other to eat, it comes to that. But water, I don't think you last more than a few days without that. Then Rep, he comes in, he takes your money, your clothes, your fine guns, along with your horses, and he's a rich man, yes. Rich enough to go back to Andorra and live like a king."

"It was Sam Volksmacht's wanting to live like a king back home that got us into this, you look at it close," someone muttered behind Faro. He recognized Slick Phil Bowyer's voice. "Now this one. What d'you suppose gets into 'em?"

"What they get into, this case," Toad Dabney said in the darkness. "It's a well-known fact that screwing sheep rots the brains, and it's another that that's what sheepherders do when the time hangs heavy on their hands."

Faro struck another match, retraced his steps to his blanket, picked up his shotgun, and returned to the door. He gauged as best he could where Rep Sandoz's voice seemed to have come from, aimed, and pulled the trigger.

Shrill laughter followed the blast, as did the noise of men coming awake in the barn. "The door, the walls, they're too thick for any guns you carry in there. Even if you shot through, hit me, what good would that do you. Nobody to let you out, you wind up the same way!"

Chapter 10

In the windowless barn, night was still absolute, though the morning was far advanced. Someone with a pocket flask pulled off a sock, doused it with whiskey, and touched a match to it, providing an improvised torch that smelled vilely. By its flickering light, Faro surveyed his followers, all of whom looked at least as apprehensive as he felt.

"What we got out there is a crazy man," he said.

"Not so crazy that he hasn't managed to get a dozen sane men locked up, and nothing they can do about it," Slick Phil Bowyer said.

"Right!" a muffled voice through the door called. "Me, Rep, I'm crazy like coyote!"

"Crazy man with keen ears," Toad Dabney said.

"Thing is, what we going to do about it?" Faro said, pitching his voice lower, an example which the others followed. If they managed to think up some way out of their predicament, they did not want to make Rep Sandoz privy to their plans.

"You're the commander-in-chief, the five-star general," Porky James said.

"Well, then, I need the advice of my fucking staff, don't I?" Faro said. "Ulysses S., and Lee and them, they didn't just lay back and say, 'Less go take Vicksburg or defend Richmond,' and tell everybody how to do the job, they got information and worked out what had to be done from that."

"The roof," Jarvis said. "It's probably weaker than the door, sure to be weaker than the walls. Maybe we could break through it and get out."

Faro looked around the empty barn, devoid of ladders, timbers, or anything that might serve to get a man up to the dimly lit rafters and planks that sheltered them from the sky. Then he looked at the eleven men clustered around him. "Lemme see . . . You, Schroeder, you're the heftiest. Go over and brace yourself against the wall. Now you, Porky, clamber up onto Dutch's shoulders." When, with some grunting and protests, this had been accomplished, Jarvis was sent to try to mount the human ladder, but the result was a cursing tangle of men on the floor.

Faro next calculated that four men at the base could support three, who could support two, who could support one . . . who, if he had especially long arms, might just be able to scratch at the roof. Well, shit.

"Time to go see to my sheep," the voice from outside said. "I come back in a while, see how my two-leg sheep doing. I don't get meat from you, but I get your wool, everything you carry, soon as you die from thirst or kill each other to eat." Rep Sandoz concluded his comment with a cheerful cackle.

Dutch Schroeder, disentangled from the men who had tried to climb on his shoulders, gave a full-throated bellow of despair, like a calf feeling the knife at its throat. *"Wir sind verloren! Niemand kann uns hilfen!"*

"He praying?" Faro asked Slick Phil Bowyer, who was widely known to have a faulty knowledge of several languages.

"Old-country talk. Uh, he's saying we're done for, nobody can help us."

Faro would have liked to disagree with the sentiment, but could not.

"What's that?" Sandoz said through the door. "What'd somebody say about Nieman?"

"Oh, Lord," Faro said. "The man's trying to kill us, and, if that ain't enough, he's horning in on our last words, and them in the Dutch tongue at that. What's he—"

"Dip me in shit, roll me in corn meal and deep fry me!" Slick Phil Bowyer said excitedly. "Maybe . . . Hey, I scored big on a mark out this way one time, name of Nieman, Marcus Nieman I think it was, back in Centennial year. Owned about every sheep there was hereabouts, he did. Nine to three, this Rep works for him, and he figured that what Dutch was saying had to do with him, and it's got him shook up, hearing his boss's name coming from in here."

Faro made an instant decision. Nine-three was better odds than he'd had in a while, and there wasn't any other game in town. "Nieman's waiting for us, Sandoz!" he called. "We come on down here to buy some sheep from him. He's expecting us at his place today, tomorrow at the latest. We don't show up, he'll have men out looking for us. And they'll look in here, there'll be traces where our horses was, even if you drive 'em off. Even if he's a little late about it, and we don't make it, you're the man to look after if they find us corpsed in here. You could lose your job over this!"

There was a long silence from outside. Then Rep

Sandoz said, "I keep you in there, Mr. Nieman will be mad at me, fire me, and I can't earn at anything but sheepherding. But if I let you out, you'll kill me for shutting you up."

"For shit sure," Porky James said softly. Faro did not think it worthwhile to confute Sandoz's speculation.

"If I can't get to Andorra and be a rich man, and if I'm going to lose my job, why live? Maybe the best thing, I go hang myself from tree, leave you in there."

"Hey, that way everybody loses, Sandoz," Faro said hastily. "Less work this out." Ulysses S. Grant was never in a place like this, as far as he could recall from what he had gathered of the war, but he would likely have thought of something clever to do about it. Faro tried to think like a general, and a general in deep shit at that. "Sandoz!" he called. "Listen, is there any big rocks out there?"

"Rocks all over, what's that got to do with anything?"

"Well, hey, you're a strong man, lifting all them sheep or whatever you do. You just go hump some of them rocks over here by the door, pile 'em up against it. Some big, heavy ones, see. Then you lift up the outside bar and make off away from here. By the time we can push the door open, you'll be long gone, and there can't nobody potshoot you."

"But you'll talk to Mr. Nieman and he'll fire me?"

"What for?" Faro said. "You can tell him you thought we was cattlemen coming in to poison the sheep or something. He ain't going to fire you easy anyhow, there ain't that many men that'd come out here and do the job you do. I'll undertake we won't low-rate you to him, but even if we was to, it wouldn't cut no ice, I'd bet."

There was no reply, but after fifteen minutes, the

men in the barn heard scraping sounds outside the
door, and an occasional thump as if something heavy
had hit against the solid wood. A quarter of an hour
later, Sandoz called to them, "Enough stones, I think.
I lift the bar now. Remember, you promise you don't
say any bad things about me to Mr. Nieman."

"Won't even mention your name," Faro said.

He and the others moved to the door and began to
push.

It took ten minutes of hard work before the door
moved enough to emit a crack of light. The men
cheered at the sight of it and renewed their efforts.
When the gap had widened to a foot, Slick Phil Bowyer, the slightest of the party, took off his jacket and
wriggled through, and began working at the stones
from the outside. In a few moments, the door was
open enough so that the rest could emerge, and all
trooped out into the morning sunshine.

Faro looked around, noting thankfully that the
horses and mules were still where they had been
tethered. He scanned the surrounding hills, but could
not see the shepherd, though sheep were grazing in
scattered groups.

"Ought to hunt the bastard down and string him
up," said Dutch Schroeder, who had recovered his
composure.

Faro shook his head. "He knows the country better'n we do, and if he means to hide, he can do it. Take
a long time, and likely we wouldn't find him. Best to
get on our way."

"Shoot some of the sheep, then," Schroeder urged.
"Give him something to remember us by."

"Nieman's sheep," Faro said. "Sandoz is just the
hired man. He don't know it, but Nieman done us a
good turn, at least using his name in vain did, so
there's no call to hurt him. Anyhow, that Sandoz is

just plain crazy, both for what he aimed to do to us and for how he let us talk him out of it, and there's no percentage in getting into a fight with a crazy man."

As they lugged their belongings from the barn and began preparing for the day's journey, Toad Dabney asked Faro, "What d'you suppose sent him mad?"

"Sun, wind, being alone all the time out here, maybe."

"I still say it's screwing sheep."

A few hours later, it seemed to Faro that the climate in this part of the world would be enough to fry any man's wits. The horses were picking their way through drifts of hot sand from which the sun's heat was reflected with the effect of a furnace. Wind-scoured rocks contorted against the sky. The one mercy was that the sun was filmed, and hung balefully in a sky the hue of weathered brass; if it had been naked, he felt sure that he and the rest would have been broiled alive as they rode. The air was still and dense, and the ground ahead shimmered in the heat.

He hoped that the map was correct. It showed this patch of desert extending only a few hours' ride across their route; they should be into more hospitable country before nightfall.

Old Jeff Davis, back before the war, when he was in the government, he tried out camels for getting around in this kind of country, I recall right, Faro thought. Be handy if we had some of them to use just now.

He looked sharply ahead as something on the horizon caught his glance. Hard to make out in the heat haze, but it had the look of a town. Funny, none marked on the map here. But there seemed to be buildings, and . . . now, didn't that part over there look like Prison Hill in Yuma? Blake, you are working with cooked brains, you start getting such fancies, he told himself. "You see that ahead, Toad," he asked Dabney.

Dabney nodded. "Gave me a turn at first. But I've read about that kind of thing—mirage, something the sun does to the air, makes shapes in it, sometimes a kind of picture of a real place a long ways away. It'll go away in a minute."

Faro sighed. It was nice not to have to worry about being crazy, but it would have been nicer to be within sight of Yuma already. The heat and the stillness of the air were becoming unbearable. Well, no . . . it was still as hot, but there was at least a stir to the air now, producing the counterfeit of a cooling breeze.

The air movement picked up steadily; now feathers of sand could be seen twisting along the surface. Something rattled on his trousers, and he looked down to see wind-driven sand bouncing off his leg and his mount's flanks. The brassy color of the sky was deeper now, and the sun a touch more veiled.

"Sonofabitch!"

Faro turned at the yell from the rear of the group. Behind them a dirty-yellow cloud seemed to have descended to the ground, extending halfway to the zenith. The wind began to blow more strongly, and sand stung his face. The cloud rolled toward them at the speed of an express locomotive.

"Everybody!" he called. "Handkerchiefs or whatever out—you don't have one, rip off a piece of your shirt! Tie what you got over your face and hunch down!" Half the men were already doing this, but commanders were expected to give orders when something shitty came along. This looked like being his last one, though.

He moistened his handkerchief from his canteen and plastered it over his face, tying it behind, then jamming his hat down hard to help hold it in place. He crouched, lying forward on the horse's neck, and gripped the reins tightly.

When the full sandstorm struck, it was almost as if he were naked; he felt pelted with a thousand needles, even through the fabric of his coat and shirt. The horse screamed and reared, then ran stumbling along. Faro held on, his eyes closed tightly, feeling grit working its way through the wet handkerchief and into his nose and mouth. He tried to breathe shallowly, but all that was available seemed to be a mixture of air and sand; you couldn't get one without the other.

The horse lurched, stumbled, staggered, galloped, maddened by the assault of the storm. Faro clutched hard, for once feeling a trace of sympathy for the species. Stupid, vicious and uncomfortable to ride though they were, the brutes didn't deserve this. On the other hand, neither did he.

As far as he could guess, it was somewhere about 1903 that he felt the wind begin to subside, and the sting of the sand on his back became a patter, then died away. The horse slowed its pace to a normal walk, and the breath Faro drew through the handkerchief was almost free of grit. Cautiously, he sat upright and peeled the fabric from his face. The air was clear again, and the sand lay unmoving in its bed. Ahead, the rear edge of the storm loomed against the southern sky, then dwindled. He consulted his watch and found that the storm's duration had been only about half an hour, not decades, as it had seemed at the time.

He looked around. Two dust-colored horses and riders were within a few hundred yards of him; the others were nowhere to be seen. They spotted him at the same time, and all three cantered to join each other. Under the dust, Faro recognized Toad Dabney and Slick Phil Bowyer, who was raising clouds from his clothes as he beat at them with his hat.

"We come through it," Toad Dabney said disbelievingly.

"A quarter of us, anyhow," Faro said. "Less go up that hill over there and see can we spot the others."

The elevation revealed the location of four men and horses, who rode to where Faro and the others were, and of one of the two supply mules, which was retrieved.

"The rest must be some distance off," Faro said. "Lessee can we scrabble out some brushwood or what and touch off a fire. Air's still now, and the smoke'll go straight up, let 'em know where we're at."

The fire brought in four more men in the next hour. "Thass all of us but Schroeder and Jarvis," Faro said, "and one mule. Keep the fire going, Toad, and the rest of us'll quarter around and see if we come acrost anyone. Everybody back here by dusk, and we'll study out what to do next."

Riding to the northeast, Faro topped a rise and saw two sandy mounds, irregularly shaped. Out of one protruded the limp leg of a horse. The other was smaller. He approached it, dismounted, and brushed sand away. Dutch Schroeder's face looked peaceful, but his head lay at a sharp angle to his shoulders.

Horse broke its leg in a hole or what, threw him, neck broke when he hit the ground, Faro thought. Quick, anyways.

He hoisted Schroeder's body and slung it over the back of his horse, then rode back toward where the signal fire sent its thread of smoke into the sky.

None of the riders had come across any trace of Jarvis or the missing mule. Under the drifting sand, the soil was hard-baked, and it was a back-breaking effort to dig out a hole deep enough for Schroeder's blanket-wrapped corpse.

"You say the words, Phil," Faro told Bowyer. Commanders had responsibilities, but also the right to delegate them, and acting as an impromptu preacher was not something he wanted to do, or could. No disrespect to the cloth, but a con man, with his gift for words, made a pretty fair stand-in.

Slick Phil said something that sounded to Faro reasonably like what he had heard at regulation funerals, making Dutch sound better than he had been in life, the way they always did, and, playing the odds, getting in something about Jarvis, who was either making his way out of the desert on his own or turning into a mummy some place, with the smart money being placed on the last proposition.

Schroeder's body was lowered into its shallow grave, sand was pushed over it, and laboriously gathered stones piled up over it.

The evening was cool and revivified the survivors. After supper, Faro said, "Listen, all. This is a shitty place to be, and the sooner we're out of it, best for us. We been through a lot today, but I say we move on now, even though it's night. Horses can find their way, we can stay awake enough to keep in the saddle, and we'll be out of this come sunup. We'll be in the foothills of the Black Mountains by then, and we can rest ourselves there. Going by the map, there's water and trees and so. And for sure, no sandstorms and heat. Less just move on."

Riding along at the head of the procession, glancing over his shoulder from time to time to make sure that the star at the end of the Dipper was just about behind him, Faro remembered Cassie Tabard's prophecy, spat out in anger at her father's stronghold. True enough so far, a damned hard piece of traveling, and not everybody making it.

Chapter 11

Through the night, moving slowly and letting the horses find their footing in the sandy waste, the party crossed the arm of the desert. As the stars paled, something loomed ahead and on the left, gaining definition in the predawn light.

"That'll be the Blacks," Faro told Toad Dabney. "Out of this in not much longer."

Just at dawn, the horses' hoofs stopped crunching on sand and gave the familiar thud of contact with compact earth. Soon the scent of foliage came to them. One tree appeared, then a group of them at the top of a knoll. When they reached them, Faro reined up and waved his men to a halt.

"Far enough for tonight," he said. "We'll sleep here, move on when we're rested. By the map, there's a town about six hours' ride from here, so tonight we can maybe find us a place to stay, get some of the sand and shit washed off of us."

His followers saw to their horses, then lurched away

dragging blankets, and were almost all asleep within a minute of their hasty bivouacking.

Faro awoke a little before noon and found that Porky James was up and working over a cookfire. "Mule that was lost had all the bacon on it, and the canned stuff," he reported, "but we still got the coffee, and what's left of the beef from Herriman, and a few eggs. If they weren't baked in their shells in the heat yesterday, I'll fry 'em along with steaks. But that's about the last of the food, except for some flour. Fried dough's all we can come up with 'til we find a place where we can get some more."

At breakfast, Faro studied the map taken from Three-Balls Tabard's wall, what seemed like a lifetime ago. The route through the foothills of the Black Mountains seemed straightforward enough, but there was a lot maps didn't show, he knew. "Anybody know anything about this area?" he asked.

A man named Emmett said, "Me and Walsh here, we did some trapping hereabouts a while back. Not this particular place, but we got some notion of the feel of it."

"Okay, less you and him and me scout on ahead a little, make sure we're on the right track, before all of us get going. Couple places here, it ain't all that clear which way to go when."

The three men, Faro carrying Slick Phil Bowyer's glasses, rode south for half a mile, then topped a rise. The country was sparsely treed, but after the deadly desert of the previous day, it seemed like dense forest. Below and to the left he saw a stream and made a mental note to check the water barrels; probably they could use some refilling.

Movement caught his eye, and he raised the glasses. He saw a dark-skinned woman, clad only in a brief buckskin skirt, pounding clothes laid on the stream bank with a rock. He ignored the brief stirring in his loins that the sight of her breasts, swaying with the motion of her work, brought to him, and said, "Indian woman down there, there should be a camp or village nearby. Maybe we can dicker with them for some food. When you was out here, you fellows have any truck with the Indians?"

"Lots," Walsh said. "Emmett and me, we know just how to handle Injuns. We'll go on down and talk to her and get her to be friendly to us." Emmett grinned and nodded his agreement. "You just wait here, and we'll find out all you need to know."

Faro watched as the two men rode down the rise. Most of the men in the party he had known, well or slightly, in the past, but Emmett and Walsh were unfamiliar to him until their recruitment by Sam Volksmacht. He hoped that their claimed familiarity with the local Indians would pay off. It was probable that they would be able to provision fully at the next town that evening, but it was imprudent to travel through unknown country with no reserve supplies at all. Though, from his recollection of Indian cuisine, he suspected that whatever they might get from the woman's tribe would be on the order of boiled dog.

He lost Emmett and Walsh in the trees, and returned to watching the woman through his glasses. She was a little plump but a good-looker. He saw her stop her work abruptly and stare over her shoulder. He swung his glasses in the direction she was looking and observed Emmett and Walsh dismount from their horses and approach her.

Faro turned his glasses on the woman again and saw, to his surprise, that she was darting back, her eyes wide, and reaching for a rock. A fast shift of view back to the two men revealed the reason: the front of

Emmett's trousers was open and his erection was wagging as he strode toward her. Then both men grabbed her and wrestled her to the ground.

Faro ground his teeth in rage as he watched Walsh rip the woman's skirt away and push her legs apart, then move up and grab her by the torso, a hand squeezing each breast as Emmett drove into her. The woman writhed and tried to pull free, but Emmett's weight on her and Walsh's grip held her fast.

Faro cursed and ran for his horse. He mounted and started ahead, then paused. A figure had emerged from the edge of the clearing where the woman had been doing her wash, and was witnessing the scene on the bank. Faro put the glasses to his eyes, and saw an Indian in buckskin leggings. As he watched, the man pulled a war hatchet from his waist, ran swiftly forward, and with two blows brained the preoccupied Emmett and Walsh.

He stopped and rolled Emmett's corpse off the woman and pulled her to her feet. Her face and breasts were dabbled with Emmett's blood, and she rubbed it in with an expression of vengeful triumph, tracing war-paint patterns, then bent and spat on his body.

"Don't believe I'll go down there and see can I trade for food just now," Faro muttered aloud. "Doubt they're in the mood for visitors."

While the woman picked up and refastened her skirt, the man tumbled the two dead men into the river and watched them float away, then went to inspect their horses. The woman spread out another garment on the bank to dry, and returned to the river to continue with her washing.

"They ast for it, my way of thinking," Faro said to his reduced band. "I don't see we got any call to waste time with what the army calls a punitive expedition."

Fortunately, Emmett and Walsh had no close friends among the group, and the general opinion was to move on and forget the incident.

"Eases up the strain on the supplies, anyway," Porky James said.

"What's the name of this place?" Toad Dabney asked Faro. Faro consulted the map. "Sunrise."

"And we get to it at sunset, that figures. Part and parcel with the way things've been going on this jaunt."

From where they were halted, a little distance from its outskirts, Sunrise appeared to be a moderately sized town with all the amenities they would need, provided it was safe to enter it. "I best sniff ahead first," Faro said. "Old Tabard'll have set about having us hunted by now, for sure. I'll listen around in a saloon or so, see if there's any word on us going around."

"Glad to go with you," Toad Dabney said eagerly.

Faro shook his head. "A chance they'll be watching for us, and might take me. Few enough of us left, it's better to risk one than two. You and the rest keep an eye out, and if I ain't back after an hour, hour and a half, strike out around the town and keep going."

He rode ahead and entered the town. The first building at the edge, oddly isolated, was a substantial, well-kept frame house of two stories, with the blinds in the downstairs windows drawn. The whorehouse, for a bet, he thought. If it's safe for us to come in, expect the boys'll be in a fancy to pay a visit later on. Them damn fools Walsh and Emmett, they might as well of waited, it'd of cost 'em a lot less.

Ahead on the main street he saw a couple of saloon signs and made for them. Lettering on a plate-glass window proclaimed that he was passing the town marshal's office. Sweating a little, he glanced in at the man who sat behind the desk, a star on his shirt. The marshal glanced up at him incuriously and returned to his paper work.

Either he's short-sighted, or Tabard ain't put out my description this far, Faro thought with relief. Best not drop my name anywhere, though, 'til I see how the wind's blowing.

"Faro Blake!" Oh, shit, somebody's dropped it for me. He turned to look at the woman who had addressed him from the plankwalk. "Hey, Doll," he said with forced heartiness. He glanced around; luckily, nobody had been within earshot. He leaned out of the saddle toward her and said, "Listen, Doll, appreciate it if you call me something else than that for a little. It might be there's some folks around that'd be gladder to see me than I would be to see them, if you get what I mean."

"Sure thing, Henry," the woman said cheerfully. Doll Falkayne had once worked for Nell, and, like her employer in the past, had gathered enough capital to start in business on her own. She was professionally used to having many of her acquaintances travel under a variety of names. "What're you doing here, Fred?"

"Passing through, maybe. Kind of a long story. Need to get some information."

"Well, the town madam hears about everything there is to know, Arthur," Doll said. "You just ride alongside while I walk back to my place, and I'll give you a drink, and you can tell me about it and see if I know what you need to know."

Faro relished the softness of the overstuffed chair in Doll Falkayne's private room and the quality of the brandy she had provided him. He sat back and let the chair do its best to soothe away the ache of days in the saddle and nights on the ground.

"I haven't heard of anything like that," Doll Falkayne said. She was a tall, rangy woman with a wide, humorous mouth, a strong nose and clear gray eyes; not conventionally pretty, but strikingly handsome. "I'd think if the marshal had had a message like that, I'd have known it by now. Also, I don't remember anything ever being said about him having any connection with the Tabards, not that he'd say much about it if he had. But I can find that out faster than you can."

"Well, then, maybe it's safe to come on in and find a place to stay," Faro said.

"Maybe and maybe not. All I said is that I haven't heard anything, not that there's nothing to hear. Let me see . . . there's eight of you?"

"Yeah," Faro said, sipping at the brandy.

"All right," Doll Falkayne said. "This house is a lot bigger than I need, and there's five rooms upstairs I don't use. I took it because the location's right and the rent was cheap. You bring your men in after dark, stable the horses out back, and come in by the back way. I'll have the chore girl make up two beds each in three rooms, one in the two others, and she'll bring up some suppers once you're in. That way, nobody'll see you, and you can have a place to stay until you're sure it's safe for you in Sunrise."

"Well, hey," Faro said, "that's damned nice of you, Doll. If it won't put you out—"

"Oh, I expect to be paid, and not all that cheaply, either, Blake," Doll Falkayne said. "A girl doesn't work for Nell Garvin and not learn to charge a fair price for what she's selling."

*　　　*　　　*

"Now, that is some kind of leadership," Slick Phil Bowyer said admiringly. "Send the man in to see if it's safe to come in and infest the local fleabag, and he gets us put up in a fancy whorehouse, with hot and cold running women and all, and our personal Pinkerton to nose out if there's a price on our heads here. Inspired, I call it."

"Directly I get there and get outside that supper, I'll send for a girl, no, two, and see if I can remember what women are for," Toad Dabney said. Doll Falkayne had cautioned Faro that, until she was certain how things stood, her new tenants should rely on room service for anything they required.

After dark, they approached Doll Falkayne's place from the rear, put up their horses, and entered by the back door. He went up the back stairs first, hearing the sound of talk, laughter, and a piano from the front parlor, and saw that the corridor was clear, and called his men up.

He assigned them rooms, giving himself and Toad Dabney the singles, then, as arranged, went to Doll Falkayne's private room and told her of their arrival.

"I'll tell the girl to bring up the meals," she said. "And your friends can have whatever girls they're willing to pay for. But, from what you've told me about the last couple of days, I'll bet they find a better use for their beds first."

And, when Faro went to check on his men, after finishing his meal in a fog of weariness, true enough, they were all asleep. Well, for sure they'd make up for it tomorrow.

Chapter 12

Rested after close to twelve hours' sleep and fueled by the hearty breakfast Doll provided, Faro's band proceeded to make up not only for their last night's deprivation, but also for what they had suffered on their journey so far.

Doll Falkayne's daytime business was about nonexistent, Sunrise being a hard-working town and anybody with the leisure for whoring before the end of business hours likely to be past the age of such interests. The men were therefore able to make free of the house and the girls. If free's the right word here, Faro thought, surveying the scene; Doll's totting up everything like a cash register, I bet, and it'll all be on the bill. Well, hell, the fellows can afford it, and they got the money for it. Jesus, what Porky just done'll likely jack the total up another two bucks!

"For a fat man, he's a goer," Doll Falkayne, standing next to Faro in the parlor entrance, said admiringly.

"Comes of not drinking," Faro said. "Keeps his wits clear to think up stuff."

Slick Phil Bowyer and three other men, Whitney, Brown and Robinson, had chosen to entertain girls in their rooms. Porky James, Toad Dabney, and a man called Smith had preferred the amenities of the parlor, with its ready supply of liquor and food and a piano for musical accompaniment to their activities.

Porky James, plumply pink all over, was entangled with three girls, humping away enthusiastically at one, with his head angled to one side enough for him to bury his face between the spread legs of another. His left hand explored the ample contours of a third, while his right held a ham sandwich, which he munched on from time to time.

Porky by name and porker by nature, Faro thought. A man can use a little fun now and then, all right, but no need to make a pig of hisself over it. And Toad ain't much better, nor Smith.

Toad Dabney was sitting in a wide, soft chair with his trousers around his ankles, accepting the attentions of a blonde in a loose wrapper who crouched in front of him, mouthing his erection. Two tables flanked the chair, one holding plates of food and the other a bottle of wine and a glass. With his broad mouth stretched beatifically wider, Dabney alternately ate and drank while the blonde worked dutifully away.

The music was provided by another girl who was giving a ragged performance of "Oh, Susannah" on the piano. Her efforts were a little hampered by the fact that, her skirt hiked above her drawerless waist, she was seated on Smith's lap, the central feature of which was buried in her, and his hands were sliding inside the front of her dress, squeezing in time to the music.

"My God," Doll Falkayne said. "Did you see what

the fat one just did? I don't know if I should charge him extra, or give him a discount for showing me something I never even thought of."

"What?" said Faro, who had been looking at the musician and her accompanist.

"Finished now, and I don't know that I've got the words for it. Say, you're not joining in—how come? There's still a girl or so around, if the fat one doesn't use them all up."

"Uh . . ." Shit, I'd feel like all kinds of a fool was I to say anything about the responsibilities of command and that. But it's the truth I'm in charge, and that means I got to act like a general, or anyhow a man, not a animal. For now, anyways. "It's . . . well, I'm worried about how we get the rest of the way, and it's more to the front of my mind just now than anything else, I guess. Listen, less go talk some, okay?"

In her private room, Doll Falkayne said, "First thing, I asked some of the customers last night— discreet, so there'd be no wondering what I was up to—about your problem. There was no sign of anything like that, no hint that the marshal might be looking out for any one of you or all of you. The men I asked are in a position to know, and a couple of them are the kind that would spill all they know in their cups or in bed. I think you can take it that there's no danger for you here, anyway."

"Thass good," Faro said. "Maybe Tabard ain't got the heft he thinks. Or maybe it's just that he don't have it here. Nothing to say that the next place, there won't be a cop that's aching to do the old bugger a favor. Well, that's one worry I got. And another is, I just don't know the damn country worth spit. There was a couple of fellows with us that might of, but they was the ones that went at the Indian woman and got sent downstream. So far I lost four men. Not my fault, far's

I can see, bad luck and their own pure foolishness done it, but it weights on me. There's a good ways to go yet 'til we get to Yuma, and I wisht I knew more about the kind of stuff we might run into."

Doll Falkayne sipped the glass of wine she was holding. "If you want to stay on another day—no reduced rates, but I think your people could use some more time to rest up—there might be something you could do about that."

A couple of hours' ride to the east, she explained, there was a town called Sulphur. "They used to mine it there for a while, but it ran out and the place closed down. There's still buildings and the works and so on, but it's kind of like a ghost town. Not really, because there's people living there."

After Sulphur had been abandoned by those who had made their living from the mine and the businesses it supported, the town had remained empty for a while. Then a few new inhabitants had drifted in, then others, until there was now a fair squatter population. "Old people, some that want a place to hide and can't be anywhere else, people nobody's got a use for. Some of them have some money, and some can go out and do odd jobs. There's a little good land nearby, not enough to attract a real homesteader, but they can grow enough to help feed themselves."

"I ain't proposing to put me nor the others into a old folks' home," Faro said irritably.

"No, of course not. What I'm getting at," Doll Falkayne said, "is that there are people there who could be useful to you. Some of them come in to Sunrise to buy supplies, and I've gotten to talking with them now and then. There are some old trappers, mountain men, steamboaters there, along with the rest, who don't have any place else to go, men who've been about everywhere around here. They'll know the kind of thing you want to find out. You could be out there and back by nightfall."

"I'll be damned," Faro said thoughtfully. "Hey, that does sound like a good idea. Good or bad, it's a idea, anyways, which is more than what I got on my own. You want to tell me how to get to this Sulphur place?"

"Sure. But, one thing, it'd be a good idea to bring along a few bottles of good booze to help loosen their tongues. They can't afford it, and I understand that it's one of the things they really miss. I'll help you pick out some from my stock."

Another item on the bill, Faro thought. Well, anything that would help on this damn trip would be worth it.

Sulphur lay huddled in a wide crack in the earth, a clump of sagging, unpainted buildings, almost always shadowed by the sheer slopes that surrounded it. A gaping hole in one slope indicated the entrance to the abandoned mine. As Faro rode in, figures stirred on ruinous porches and stoops and drifted out to stand before him.

He had never seen so many old people in one place in his life. They looked about as used-up as anybody he remembered ever having met. Doll Falkayne had hinted at the place being a hideout for wanted men; he doubted if anyone, anywhere, wanted any of those he now saw. Even with its population, this was still a ghost town—the whole damn population looked like ghosts.

"Heydee," he said, forcing geniality. "Come to visit a spell, get the benefit of your wisdom, so to speak. Anybody care to have a drink on me while we talk about that?"

He broke out a bottle, and the Sulphurites gathered

eagerly around, passing it from one to another, both men and women drinking eagerly and seeming to regain a little animation.

Faro explained that he wanted to talk to somebody, or a few somebodies, with knowledge of the Colorado and the route between Sunrise and Yuma.

"Ah, young man," a withered, tall man with a sparse beard said, "it's a shame you don't want to know about the Mississippi instead of the Colorado. I could tell you about the Mississippi, all the way up-river from New Orleans. Rode those proud steamboats more years than I can remember, dealing faro and poker, got to know every bend and bar, every snag and sawyer, every—"

"Shut up, y'ole fool," a woman quavered, reaching yet again for the rapidly emptying bottle. "This feller's askin' 'bout the Coloradder, not the 'Sippi."

Faro looked at the old man, feeling the hair rise on his neck. "Hey, no, go on a little," he said. "I, uh, I'd like to hear some more. You ran games on the river-boats?"

"Indeed I did," the old man said. "Was one of them run out of Natchez-Under-the-Hill in the '30s, then worked out of New Orleans, upriver and down, dealing and banking, and a little con work on the side, it's safe enough to say now. Knew the best of 'em in gambling and the cons, Rountree, A. B. Blake, Helmsley, Doc Prentiss, that whole crowd. After the war times changed on the river, and I came west, worked San Francisco, Dodge, all over . . . but it all ran out on me and I just kind of dried up and blew away . . . like all of us here."

Faro looked intently at the seamed face. "You by any chance Harmon Goodale?" he asked.

"Why, yes," the old man said, beaming. "How'd you know?"

"Heard of you," Faro said, speaking with sudden difficulty against an obstruction in his throat. He remembered back a long time, to a day when, no more than thirteen, he had lounged on the deck of a riverboat and watched his father and a tall, vigorous man demonstrating variants of the Louisville Shuffle to each other while the smoke from the stacks drifted toward the brilliantly green east bank of the river. He could still hear his father saying, "Harmon, you better get that right or don't do it at all, or you'll get yourself gutshot some night."

Well, that hadn't happened, after all. The laughing, handsome gambler had survived the hazards of his trade to . . .

"Honor to meet you, Mr. Goodale," Faro said with an effort. "Hey, now I better find me somebody that can give me word about the Colorado and such. Here, keep the bottle."

Another bottle bought him the services of a shaky but sharp-witted guide, who introduced him to men who had explored the country fifty years ago or worked shallow-draft steamers from the poisonous mudflats of the Gulf to Fort Yuma and beyond and were now grounded and rotting here, the tides of their lives at full ebb. As much enlivened by talking with someone from outside as by the drink Faro provided, they gave him what information they could—trails, water holes, springs, where the river could be navigated, and the hazards that could be expected—with a clarity that he found surprising. On Three-Balls Tabard's map, which he had brought with him, he jotted down what he was told.

"Glad to talk to you," he said to the last man he consulted, having taken his final notes. "Kind of you to help me. Best be going on now."

"Might be you'll be back," the old man said. "Get

old, run out of money, run out of people who give a shit about you, Sulphur's the kind of place you wind up in. Your own kind, enough to scrape by on, it ain't that bad. Well, it is, but it's all there is by then. Don't expect I'll be around to see you, though."

Riding away, Faro felt that he had got what he had come for, so the trip had been worthwhile. But the town and the wraiths that inhabited it had shaken him. It all comes to that, what's the sense in living in the first place? he wondered.

Chapter 13

"I got to thank you," Faro told Doll Falkayne. "Some of that stuff them old-timers told me can come in handy. But a place like that, it's kind of undoing to see. I don't aim to peg out young, but getting old like that, and winding up in a place like that, it don't encourage a man to keep at it."

"Well, you didn't peg out young, did you?" Doll Falkayne said. "Neither did I. Check a calendar some time."

I'm still a year or so shy of forty, Faro thought. That's . . . shit, no, it ain't. Not Harmon Goodale time yet, but that's in sight a ways down the line.

"Boys behaved themselves while I was gone?" he asked.

"Sure. Or, more likely, wore out," Doll Falkayne said. "The fat one did something you wouldn't credit with two girls and some barbecued ribs the chore girl cooked up, but then his boiler ran out of steam or something, and he's been sleeping like a babe most of the afternoon. I'd say that your people have worked off whatever they'd built up on the trip by now."

"Good. Since it seems to be safe, I'll go out tomorrow and get what we need for the rest of a trip, buy a pack mule if I can, and we'll push on. Shouldn't be more'n a couple of days before we hit the river at a place where some kind of boat can take us on down to Yuma. And then the whole shooting match will be done with, thank God."

"And Nell Garvin's there, you say."

"Yeah, and setting up to be a propertied woman, along of being in the trade you and her is at."

"Give her my regards, and tell her I hope she gets everything she's after," Doll Falkayne said, with something in her eyes Faro did not quite understand. "She's not an easy woman to understand, but there's a lot more to her than you might think, and I owe her a good bit for what she taught me. Now, you, Blake. With everything you've gone through, you must be tuckered out. Do you want to go up to your room, have the chore girl bring you some supper, and hit the hay, get ready for starting up tomorrow?"

Faro considered the days on the trail, the dangers, the loss of his men, the encounter with the denizens of Sulphur and the chilling effect it had had—and, for some reason, Doll Falkayne's mention of Nell Garvin, though that didn't seem to fit in—and said, "Well, after."

"After what?"

"After we fuck, Doll."

Doll Falkayne smiled broadly. "Blake, I have to admire you. Finally you've hit on something I'm not going to charge you for."

Doll Falkayne slid sweat-slick thighs on Faro's upper leg and grunted with pleasure as she clamped and

slackened them. Her slickness moistened the surface
of his skin as she straddled him. "Hey, I ain't going to
be no more good to you for a hell of a time," he said.
"I emptied out the fambly jewel safe pretty complete,
back there."

"Mmm," Doll Falkayne purred. "Don't worry
about it. 'S my job. Just lie back there this time."

Never seen a woman with big bones and big tits
before, Faro thought, watching Doll Falkayne's
breasts sway as she rode his thigh, eyes closed and her
lower lip caught in her teeth. Now, Nell, her tits are
about the same size, but kind of nicer-looking, but
they go along with a kind of mingier build. What Doll
and me just done, that was pretty damn fine, but not so
fine's some times with Nell. . . .

Doll Falkayne gave a contented sigh and rolled away
from him. She laid one hand on his limp penis and
grinned at him, then pinched gently. "You want to
know what your fat friend did with those barbecued
ribs? Or what the one that looks like a frog got up to
with Sandra and Oline?"

"Okay," Faro said. Since there was no immediate
likelihood of continuing what he had been up to with
Doll, he might as well hear some funny stories.

Doll Falkayne stroked him lightly as she recounted
the culinary and sexual exploits of Porky James, and
something really remarkable that Toad Dabney had
managed. By the time her account was finished, the
combination of the narrative and her fondling had
returned him to effectiveness—a lot sooner than he
had expected.

"Welcome back," Doll Falkayne said.

"Make that welcome aboard," Faro said, sliding
aside, turning over, and placing himself atop her.
"And, like they say in the navy, prepare to receive

boarders." With more than the usual pleasure of the action, he parted the softness between her legs with his fingers and drove into her. Screw you, Harmon Goodale, he told himself. I got a long road to travel before I wind up where you are. Doll Falkayne gave a birdlike cry of pleasure and clutched him to her.

By late morning of the next day, Faro had purchased the supplies he estimated would be needed for the rest of the journey, seen to their loading on the remaining original mule and the one he had bought in Sunrise, and exacted from his rested followers their shares of the amount—large, but not exorbitant—that Doll Falkayne had asked for their keep and the use of her staff. He contemplated shaving the substantial stubble that had sprouted on his chin, sparser than his mustache, but looking close to intentional, and decided against it. It would be a needless chore on the trail, and, if anybody in Tabard's pay should be on the lookout for him, a beard might be a kind of disguise.

"You might want to go back the way you came," Doll Falkayne told him, "then cut around town to the east and hit the south track later on—it'd take an hour or so extra. There's a noon social at the Methodist Church, and there'll be a lot of people out for it. Eight men riding through, it would attract attention, and if Three-Balls Tabard ever does get through to here, it'd put him after you."

"The hell with that," Porky James said, when Faro relayed her suggestion to his men. "They don't know about us yet, ma'am, as you've told us, and if we get over to the river and onto a boat, we'll be where it doesn't matter pretty soon. I say, let's just boil through, instead of going roundabout. I vote we ride direct."

The others backed him, and Faro, himself not much caring for more time on the trail than absolutely necessary, agreed, though with some misgivings.

To his relief, though the party attracted the glances that might be expected in reaction to a group of anonymous strangers, there was no sudden start of recognition, no quick scuttling off down the street to the marshal's office. The spire of the church showed at the far end of Sunrise, about as far from the center of town as Doll Falkayne's place, which made sense, Faro figured. As they approached it, the doors were open and the sound of singing and organ music came to them. The social Doll Falkayne had mentioned must have gone into its musical phase.

Smith, riding alongside Faro, looked toward the church and said, "That gets to me." The singers inside were giving as spirited a rendition of "Rock of Ages" as the tune allowed.

"Noticed yesterday you was fond of music," Faro said, recalling Smith's antics with the piano player.

Smith looked at him reproachfully. "Don't mock. That hymn, it brings to mind when I was a boy back in Iowa and studying pharmacy at Grinnell College. Church services every Sunday and most Wednesdays, and I was the better for it, before I fell into wild ways and left off my schooling and took up with bad companions."

"Like us?" Faro said acidly.

Smith nodded dolefully. "Just now, hearing them people singing that good old song, it came all over me. Drinking, whoring, gambling, living the way I've been, look what it's led to. Signing on with Volksmacht, then this trip. I could be dealing out pills for any and all complaints back some place where there's trees and water, respected, a family and all that."

"Well, you didn't, and that's that," Faro said. "You

picked your trail, and for now it's the same as ours, bad company or not, so less get on with riding it."

Smith shook his head. "No. That hymn's a sign to me. I've been on the wrong path, but it's not too late to change." He halted his horse, and the rest of the company drew up next to him, looking at him curiously.

"Fellows," Smith said, "the joyful noise those folks in there are raising unto the Lord has done its work with me. The scales are fallen from my eyes, and it's time to lay down my burden of sin." As his former companions gaped, he continued, "I'm going to go in there and join in, and I'm going to ask forgiveness, and I'm going to find me a new life, right here. Tabard doesn't know me by name, so I'm not worried, even if he ever does get his word to here. I am casting off the corrupt body, and that includes you fellows. No offense intended."

"None taken," Faro said faintly, as Smith reined his horse aside, dismounted, and tethered it at the hitching rail in front of the church.

They all watched him enter through the welcoming doors. "Hell," Faro said after a moment. "We best move on. They strike up Old Hundredth, likely half the rest of you'll desert."

As the depleted band resumed its progress, Faro reflected that there seemed to be a hell of a lot of ways to lose men on an expedition like this, some that Ulysses S. Grant probably never thought of.

Wonder if Smith really has turned over a new leaf? If he ain't, the lady that plays the church organ could be in for some interesting practice.

"There is something," Slick Phil Bowyer, riding beside Faro toward sunset, said.

"There is always something," Faro said.

"Behind us," Slick Phil said.

Faro turned and saw a flicker of motion on the skyline.

"Been studying that out," Slick Phil said. "I make it out to be two riders, keeping about the same distance behind us, last hour or so. They're far enough back so's it doesn't look as if they're meaning to catch up with us for company anytime soon."

"Then following," Faro said. "Fellows from Sunrise, like." By now, the habit of responsibility was ingrained in him, and he had become used to seeing right off what shit was laid out and diving into it. "It comes dark, I'll double back and see if I can find out what they're at."

It seemed to Faro that he could hear the stones crackling as they gave up the heat that they had accumulated during the day as he crept toward where the following riders had been seen at the last moment before darkness fell. He had ridden back about two miles, then tethered his horse to a stone and gone ahead on foot. There was no flickering warmth to indicate the presence of a cookfire, which was a pretty fair indication that the men Slick Phil had discerned were not innocent trail riders.

But without that fiery clue, it was damned hard to figure out where the followers had stopped for the night. Faro sniffed the night air, and got a whiff of horse, then heard a low murmur. Unless there were tourist parties coming through this desolate place, not very likely, he was close to the men who had cut their trail, and so in a fair way of finding out what they were up to.

Men's voices clarified as he scrabbled his way across the rocky ground. Half the starry sky was blacked out, and he realized that the men he hoped to eavesdrop on were ensconced in a cave in the face of a shaly cliff.

"When do we take 'em?" he heard a voice say.

"T'morrer, about first light. Behind them bluffs, we can work close in, and pick off most of 'em before, as the rest know what's happening. Be a big thing for us, old Tabard knows we done him this kind of favor. I tell you, when that key started clicking out this stuff, I never expected this kind of chance would come of it."

Okay, Faro told himself. I find my way back to the fellows, and I get us moving out fast in the night, and we keep ahead of these cannibals. He turned, and his foot slipped on a stone, sending up a rattling that echoed through the night.

He wondered briefly if Smith or Doll Falkayne had betrayed him and the men he was responsible for, then assimilated what he had overheard—no treachery, just the benefits of modern technology. Tabard, once out of his temporary imprisonment, was able to put out the word that there would be something in it for anyone who would kill or capture a bunch of hapless grifters and gamblers making their way down the Colorado. Then he moved off as rapidly as he could.

The two men in the cave were alert to the sounds he made. Flame bloomed in the dark, and a slug whined off a rock not two feet away from him.

The other man's gun joined in, and lead sang past Faro's head. He hurled himself to the broken ground and pulled his shotgun from under his coat, aiming and firing both barrels as quickly as he could.

He had hoped to hit or discourage the trackers, but the results of his shots were beyond what he expected. The loose rock fronting the cave twitched under the force of his pellets, then slid. With a roar, the front of the rock face subsided to the ground.

Unless the telegraph line ran a lot farther down than Sunrise, Faro thought, there wouldn't be much more trouble from Three-Balls Tabard. Fine—there was enough trouble along the way as it was without that.

Chapter 14

Faro looked up from Three-Balls Tabard's annotated map and scanned the sunbaked waste to the south. "Looks like this's it," he told Toad Dabney. "Them old-timers tole me about a bunch of canyons that cuts our path hereabouts, and that looks like the first of'em, about a mile on. Not awful wide, but hell to get acrost, being steep up and down. Lose one horse in three trying it, they said, though mules can do it pretty well. Best thing is to cut along over the rim and pick our way down the river, move along there for a few miles, and then get on up to the top again, where the traveling'll be easier. Or we could angle over about ten miles east, where the canyons can be crossed, then come on back here and follow the trail south. Mean a extra some hours on the way, but safer than going by the river trail, 'cause you got to be real careful if you ain't going to be dumped in, and, the way the water is hereabouts, it'd be all up with you."

"Let's go the river way," Toad Dabney said. "I'll go

saddle-crazy if I have to spend any time I don't have to on this trip. Besides, it'll be good to look at water, a whole lot of water, going by all at once. Make me feel cool just to see it."

The rest of the party agreed with Dabney. "Okay," Faro said. "Now, lessee, there should be two needly-looking rocks standing about ten feet high, on a ways. That marks the start of the best trail down the cliff to the river."

"Then we can just hang around when we get down to the river, wait for a boat to come by, and hail her?" Whitney wanted to know.

"Uh-uh," Faro said. "Boats don't work this stretch. Where it ain't rapids and falls, it's sandbars. Head of navigation's some ways on still."

He pondered the best arrangement for the traverse of the hazardous cliff trail. "Single file, me first. You, Brown, you bring up the rear, get a rope on them mules so's you can lead 'em along after us."

The first minutes of descent brought relief to the riders. As the cliff face rose above them, it cut off the sun, bringing them into shade that seemed twenty degrees cooler, and resting their eyes from the constant glare. The bank on the other side of the river glowed in the fierce sunlight, making the shadows they rode in all the more pleasurable by contrast.

The footing was not alarmingly bad, but Faro was aware of an occasional misstep and near-stumble as his mount placed a hoof on a bed of loose rock. He glanced backward. Because of the drop in the trail, he could clearly see the end of the line of riders, with the two pack mules placidly following Brown. They seemed less nervous and uncertain than the horses, in spite of the load of supplies they carried, and found their way with inborn unconcern.

The sound of the horses' hoofs on rock and the

jingle of harness began to be mingled with, then over-whelmed by a rushing sound from below. Faro looked down to his right, and saw a white streak, partly masked by some sparse greenery. Toad Dabney, just behind him, said, "Looks of that, you're right about boats. But it's damn nice to see and hear it. We got water enough to drink, but riding in that sun and all, it gets me kind of dried out in the mind, and it's good to be reminded that there's such a thing as too much water somewhere."

About fifty feet above the river, the ledge they had followed down from the rim leveled out, which was good, and narrowed by half, which was not so good. Faro sent his horse slowly ahead, silently urging it to be damned careful about where it put its feet. His right boot swung over the edge of the trail, the left from time to time scraped the near-vertical cliff face. The rock was weathered, and disposed in broken slabs, creating miniature caves. Though now in shadow, it had ab-sorbed the sun's heat through the morning hours, and was now radiating the warmth it had collected.

Faro kept an anxious eye on the route ahead. It had been twenty years or more since his informant in Sulphur had been this way, and the ledge trail could have been blocked at any point. If that was the case, they'd have to turn back and take the grinding long way around. But they couldn't do that unless they found a wide enough place on the trail to get the horses reversed without sending them over the edge. So far, it looked like there wouldn't be any such places.

Suddenly, he heard a shrill cry from the rear of the line. "Shit, oh, shit!"

He swiveled his head. The trail bulged out a little toward the river there, and Brown and his horse were clearly in view. Brown swayed in the saddle, clutching his throat. Then Faro saw something thin whip out from the crevices in the cliff and hit at Brown's cheek. At the same time he was aware of a buzzing sound, and registered the fact that whatever had struck at Brown was decorated with a diamond pattern.

Brown shrieked, wrenched himself from the saddle, fell heavily to the stony trail, skidded over the edge, and was lost to sight. In a few seconds, something bobbed briefly in the raging river and vanished.

Time seemed to have frozen, and Faro was aware of several things at once. One was that the buzzing sound had increased in volume. Another was that Brown's riderless horse was rearing and backing, its eyes rolling in panic. Behind it, the sure-footed mules were neatly executing a turn and picking their way away from the sudden disturbance. The last item of interest he registered was a stirring and writhing in the deep shadows of the narrow caves in the cliff face.

There was no chance of turning the horses, getting past Brown's maddened animal to chase the mules; there was no staying here, with God knew how many rattlers waking and considering what to do about the passing strangers; and it was near-suicide to move on at speed on this perilous trail. Well, near-suicide was better odds than going for the sure thing. "Ride like hell!" he called, and spurred his horse.

Showers of stone and dust spun out from under its hoofs, seeming to Faro to hang for a moment before they vanished; at times the river looked to be directly under him, and only the thud of the hoofbeats reassured him that they were not already falling to destruction. The ride jolted and bruised him, but there was something heady in this crazy charge to safety that exhilarated him. Just like going up against the Tabards, he thought. I ain't careful, this shit could get to be a habit.

He realized after a while that the cliff surface to his

left was smooth and solid, affording no rooming facilities for rattlesnakes, and reined up at a wide place in the trail. His followers slowed, then stopped their mounts. All sat, breathing heavily, for a moment. Faro counted them. "Six, counting me," he said. "So nobody went over on that run, thank God."

Whitney said slowly, "Shouldn't we maybe try to work our way down to the river, see can we find Brown? Maybe he's—"

"He's a dead man," Slick Phil Bowyer said. "If he didn't get torn up on the rocks, he drowned. And if he didn't drown, he's dead anyway. Two rattler bites, face and throat. Even if he was here and still living, what'd you do about it? Put a tourniquet around his neck?"

"I don't see as we're that much better off," Robinson said gloomily. "We got water with us, and we can find some water holes along the way, I expect. But with the mules gone, we don't have what to eat—and I don't think that map of yours shows any towns anywheres near here, Blake."

"True enough," Faro said. "But we'll likely come across something, maybe a ranch house, maybe a trading post that ain't marked. If we don't, soon, then we just tighten our belts and keep on. We've had the sand and the luck to keep going this far."

The other four men glanced at him, then looked away, but not so quickly that he could not read the message: just half of us that started.

They sheltered for the rest of the afternoon at the end of the trail just below the cliff rim, grabbing what sleep they could. "With no food, we got to keep up our strength," Faro said. "Uses you up less to travel in the cool, and we can find our way well enough, now there's a moon from just after sundown. Come dawn, we'll start looking for a place to hole up for the day.

All these damn rocks and canyons and such, we can find a place that'll be in shade most of the time, then go on when it's cooler."

The first night's travel worked out as Faro had predicted, and they were able to rest during the day in comparative shade, only having to wake twice to move out of the sun's course. The men were too tired to complain overmuch about the absence of food.

When they woke, got to their feet and stared at the last of the sun, Faro could sense that the mood was different. His stomach was grumbling with impatience at its emptiness, and so, he was sure, were the others'. Was someone else running this show, he thought, I'd sure as hell be mad at him and want him to do something about it. But there just ain't nothing else to do but what I'm doing.

"All right," he called with forced briskness, "less mount and ride. Sooner we're on our way, sooner we're wherever we're going."

He turned to his horse. From behind him, a voice muttered, "There's six that's got there already."

Faro whirled. "Anybody wants to take the shortcuts those fellows used is welcome. Just chew on the muzzle of your shooter and pull the trigger. You want to get out of this, follow me. You elected me to the job, and I done my best. Anybody thinks he's got a better idea how to go from here, stand for office and I won't make no stump speeches for reelection."

"We could . . ." Slick Phil Bowyer said, then fell silent. "Ah, hell, I guess it's the only thing. For now."

The inside of Faro's head seemed to be filled with a first-class San Francisco fog, but his eyes continued to observe and report on the landscape ahead, erratically lit by the moon, now far down in the west. The night's ride, after no food for two days and troubled sleep, had wearied him beyond anything he could remember; but there was nothing to do but keep going. Soon, he thought blearily, we're going to have to hunt out a place to spend the day; sky's just a touch lighter in the east, sunup can't be far off. He closed his eyes to see if he could think of any other course to follow. Maybe . . .

He opened them abruptly at Toad Dabney's soft call. "Hey." The eastern sky was noticeably brighter than it had been just a second ago . . . No, not just a second, he must have dozed in the saddle for half an hour. Some leader, Blake. "Hey what?" he asked Dabney.

"Listen. Smell."

Faro frowned. There was no particular noise; less so than usual, in fact, as the clatter of hoofs on rock was oddly muted. Then he was aware of a light swishing sound as they moved ahead, and a distinctive, off-sweet smell.

He leaned over, grasping the saddlehorn to keep from falling, and reached down; there was a soft brushing against his fingers. "We're riding through grassland, by God," he said. "Forage for the horses, and likely water around somewheres."

"More than that," Toad Dabney said jubilantly. "Grass means cattle, and cattle means ranchers, and ranchers mean ranch houses. And ranch houses mean food!"

As the news was understood by the rest of the band, they gave hoarse, croaking cheers.

The just-risen sun flooded the land with light, showing it to be an almost-flat stretch of grass, not the rich grazing lands found further east, but hardy, enduring feed all the same. The first scrawny longhorn they saw, head down and chewing and rolling its eyes for an unanxious look at them, raised another cheer. "More cows soon, then cowboys, then an escort to the ranch house, and then a damn big breakfast," Porky James said. "Those ranchers, they eat well, and there's always a meal for the passing stranger. Maybe flapjacks to start, with plenty of butter and some blueberry jam if they have it. And then about a pound of bacon each—"

"I would favor doughnuts to open," Slick Phil Bowyer said. "Coffee with lots of cream and sugar, and a nice, greasy doughnut to dip into it."

"Pie," Robinson said. "When I was a boy in New Hampshire, we always had pie for breakfast. Some sliced ham after, if we wanted feeding up for the haying or so."

Faro's preferred breakfast was an egg beaten up in brandy, but he was prepared to concede that the others' suggestions had merit, and that it might, the host's stores being capable of providing it, make sense to try one of them. Or all of them.

He mounted a little rise and saw ahead a shallow creek meandering cross the flat land, some cottonwoods growing alongside it. "Let's stop there," he called. "Get ourselves some shade, water, stick our feet or what in the crick. We can wait 'til some cowpokes happen by, or, when we're a bit rested, some of us can go out scouting for 'em."

By midmorning, the heat, even in the thin shade of the trees, was oppressive. No riders had appeared, only several cows drifted by.

"Lot of beef on that one," Porky James said hungrily, eyeing an animal grazing a hundred yards off. "No great trick to shoot it, butcher it, and have steaks frying in about no time."

"Hey," Faro said, alarmed. "These ranchers, they don't go for that stuff. Folks that run their cattle or such are likely to get about four inches taller all of a sudden, along of being stretched out by a noose."

"Who's to do the stretching?" Slick Phil Bowyer said bitterly. "We've been waiting here for hours for one of the hands to show up. I say we give ourselves a feed like Porky says and move on. We can carry enough of the meat so it'll hold us for two days."

"Well, damn it, no!" Faro said. "Thass plain crazy. After all you been through, it don't make sense, just 'cause you're a little peckish, to chance getting lynched. You leave them cows alone, and thass an order."

"Piss on your orders, Blake," Slick Bowyer said. "We're starving men, and we'll take what we need. And, considering what's happened to us so far, I don't know that any of us'll feel like taking any more orders from you."

Well, now I know how Knifelips Hogan felt, Faro thought. And I got a hell of a lot better cause than what he had, at that. I busted my ass to bring these fuckers through, and now they don't give a shit. I ain't giving up on it without another try, though.

"Listen," he said. "What I'll do, if you fellows is too spent for it yourselves, is, I'll ride out south and west, making the best time I can, hunting around for range riders, or camps or what. Lemme have your glasses, Phil, so's I can spot anything at a distance, and I'll give it, oh, two hours. I ain't found nothing or nobody by then, okay, I'll come back, you get on with the plan, and vote yourselves in a new general. I'll abide by it, and go along with everything the man says."

"All right," Slick Phil Bowyer said after a brief

conference with his fellows. "We're about crazy with hunger, but we'll give you the two hours. After that, it's steak for lunch, no matter what."

The sun was directly overhead as Faro approached the grove of cottonwoods. Just about two hours, he was thinking, and not a sight of a ranch hand to show for it. Now the thing I got to do is, I got to talk a little more persuasive, get 'em to hold off a little on the butchering plan and . . . Oh, shit on it all the way to hell, the sonsabitches jumped the gun on me! The wind had brought him the smell of broiling beef.

He spurred his horse ahead, then reined it to a halt as the sound of a gunshot came to him. The trees screened what was happening from his view, but it seemed like a lousy idea to ride any closer to whatever was going on. He dismounted, found a slight depression in which to conceal his horse, ground tied, grabbed his toolcase, and ran crouching toward the trees. No time to get out the shotgun, but it would be best to have it with him. Once he was to the trees, he could get it out, load it, and act as seemed most appropriate.

Out of breath, he came to the grove and pressed to its edge. Across the stream, about a hundred yards off, he could see a group of men, some mounted, some not. What was going on was clear enough without Slick Phil Bowyer's glasses, but, for greater detail, he brought them up to his eyes.

A butchered calf lay next to a fire on which slabs of meat sizzled, stretched on green sticks set in forked branches. Slick Phil Bowyer, Toad Dabney, Porky James, Whitney and Robinson stood with their hands tied behind their backs. Three dismounted men in the garb of range hands covered them with rifles; there were six others sitting their horses, four of them brandishing revolvers. Where was you fellows when I needed you? Faro thought bitterly.

As he watched, his last five followers were hoisted onto their horses and slung across them, the dismounted hands swung back into their saddles, and the caravan moved off.

Faro had no idea what he could do about the situation, but figured that, if he shadowed them at a distance, he might be able to work out some way to intervene in what looked like a very bad fate for the men who had trusted him—even though what was happening to them was the consequence of their letting him down when he had trusted them.

However, when he arrived where he had left his horse, the animal was nowhere in sight, even with the aid of Slick Phil Bowyer's glasses.

There was no way to follow his band and their captors on foot. Nothing, in fact, to do but get on his own way and hope that they might somehow survive. Slick Phil Bowyer had the reputation of being able to talk his way out of anything; Faro hoped it was justified.

He made his way to the deserted campfire, where the chunks of meat still cooked, grabbed one, and took it to the shelter of the trees before cutting it up with his penknife and devouring it.

"Still nice and rare on the inside," he muttered aloud, though there was no one to hear him. "Poor buggers must of hardly got it done on one side before them fellows come and took them. Can understand how the notion for it would get to them, though—don't believe I've had a meal tasted as good, no matter that the circumstances ain't ideal."

He looked at the hide of the butchered animal and shuddered. It bore a brand in the shape of a circle with stubby lines radiating from it. Of all the cattlemen they might have despoiled, his men had had to come up against old Sonnenschein, master of the Sun Ranch, who was credited with at least a score of dead rustlers. There goes the last of my command. Ulysses S. Grant never got that low, I guess. Well, there's still Faro Blake to see to.

Keeping a wary eye in the direction in which the riders had vanished, he cooked another slab of meat to a dryness which he hoped would preserve it, wrapped it in grass, stuck it in the side pocket of his jacket, picked up his toolcase, and struck out south and west on foot.

Chapter 15

"Five days more, Miss Garvin," Howard Barber said. "And that's a good bit beyond what we have to give you by law, I have to say. We could take you over for taxes and your delinquent notes any time, but we gave our word."

Gave your word, and got free booze, free food and free rides along of it, Nell thought. Her creditors had, as she had suspected they would, taken to dropping in any hour and availing themselves of her house's culinary, bibacious and sexual facilities when and as they chose. Once the arrangement had been arrived at, there had been no thought of reaching into their well-filled pockets to pay for what they received. She looked past Barber to where Asa Mosby was digging into a mound of roast beef on the sideboard, swigging a goblet of whiskey, and eyeing the lineup of girls in the parlor. Mosby was making a fortune on the food concession for the infamous territorial penitentiary on Prison Hill—of each dollar in the prisoners' food budget, as appropriated by the legislature, fifty cents went to Mosby, twenty-five to the warden and other officials, and twenty-five to the purchase and preparation of food for the inmates. This whole damn crowd should be in there, eating off of old Asa's bounty, not mine, she thought.

Still, they got me over a barrel. "I am sure that in five days' time, my partner, Mr. Blake, will be back, and will be able to meet any and all obligations from the assets which you know very well that he has," she said.

"Go on hoping," Howard Barber said with a grin.

Nell probed for something that would give her an edge, something that would at least keep these coyotes at bay for the full term they had promised but might renege on. "I'd be pleased if you and the others would be my guests at supper, the night after next," she said. "You've seen how the place operates, but you gentlemen who have a monetary interest in it, you haven't seen everything about it. I am sure that I can show you some things you weren't expecting."

"We always like the unexpected, so long as it's on the pleasant side," Barber said. "I'm sure I and my colleagues will be glad to accept your invitation, Miss Garvin."

"It's a lot to ask, I know, Ina," Nell said. "But you know how things are. It'll be a help, keep 'em off my back 'til as I can work things out. Still . . ."

"Don't worry, Miss Nell," Ina said. She was a robust brunette with flesh pleasingly disposed on a large-boned frame. "Seven at a time's no problem for me. When I was in San Diego, they called me Ironclad Ina, and it wasn't after the ships the sailors was on, neither. I've done seven in half an hour, and kept going 'til sunup. Even if it did leave me walking spraddle-legged for a day, it'd be worth it not to find myself working for any one of that bunch."

Nell's dinner party for her creditors was a good deal beyond the best Yuma could provide. The main ingredients were local, but she drew on her store of gourmet canned goods, hoarded since their purchase in San Francisco, and on her expertise in putting together something that would exceed anything her guests had experienced. A patron in Chicago, years ago, had taught her how to marinate tough fresh beef into something succulent and memorable; Tsai Wang in San Francisco had given her the knowledge that enabled her to transform the creeping and hopping things gathered from the mudflats below Yuma into a tasty soup. She rifled her cellar of the wines she kept in case any patron with an educated palate should come by, and saw to it that every man's glass was constantly topped up.

"Hey, now, what's for dessert?" Howard Barber called, belching as he finished the last of the cheese that had followed the meat course.

"Better than what my clients are getting, I'd say," Asa Mosby guffawed.

By right, Mosby, Nell thought, you and every man else here ought to be up on Prison Hill and eating what you dish out. You wouldn't have that potbelly on a quarter a day, for sure. She forced a smile and said, "Ripe peach in champagne, gentlemen."

"I don't know of any peach orchards around here," said Tod Carson, one of the minor creditors.

"Special variety," Nell said. She clapped her hands once. The chore girl hurried in with a tray laden with silver cups which she set in front of each guest, then scuttled out again.

"We're supposed to drink from these?" Howard Barber said. "Where's the champagne?"

"And the peach?" Asa Mosby said.

"Along in a minute," Nell said.

Both doors to the parlor in which the dinner was being held were thrown open, and the chore girl and Beefy Bertha, the burliest of Nell's stable of operatives, appeared, pushing in a portable zinc bathtub outfitted with rollers. It was filled with a golden liquid which fizzed at the surface with countless tiny exploding bubbles. In it reclined Ina, her body only a little clouded by the sparkling wine, smiling broadly at the guests.

"There's the champagne, gentlemen, and there's your peach, ripe for the plucking," Nell said. "Go to it."

Cups clashed against each other as the diners dove for the tub and its contents. Ina squealed with a good imitation of delight as each dessert-taker realized that only one hand was needed to dip into the champagne, and that the other could be employed in testing the "peach" for ripeness.

"Plucking time," Howard Barber announced after the level of the liquid had been substantially lowered. "Here, Asa, give the lady a hand." He and Mosby lifted a giggling Ina from the tub and to the center of the table, where she lay with her legs dangling over the edge.

"I'll leave you to it," Nell said, rising. "Enjoy yourselves."

"Hey, no, Miss Nell," Asa Mosby said. "More fun with you looking on. We're going to be doing business with you, you might as well see how we do it, if you get my meaning. Money isn't everything, and there's a lot of side deals us fellows and you can work out, to make things run more smoothly, like."

Nell grimaced faintly and sat down. It was one thing to provide about any service a customer wanted, but another when bullying came into it, which was what was happening now. All right, Ina was primed for it, and she herself had accepted it as a condition of keeping going, of buying time.

Carson and Mosby held Ina's legs apart, running their hands over her body, as Barber fumbled his trousers open, freeing his erection, and drove into her.

Ina wriggled and squealed convincingly for him, as she did for Carson, shortly after. Mosby rolled her over, and drew a more heartfelt cry as he stirred her to greater activity with prods from a fork.

Nell, watching grimly, noted that the men were lined up in an order determined by the amounts to which she was indebted to them. They couldn't have worked it out in advance, she supposed; it must just come naturally to them.

"Hell," Ina said, "it wasn't that much. There was a time when all the other girls in Mother Porter's was down with the influenza, and a whaler came in after two years at sea, and only me to see to the boys." Seated in Nell's room after the departure of the guests, she sipped at a glass of brandy and drew on a cigarette, pulling her silk wrapper around her. "Now, that was some goings, and it helped me earn my nickname. But it was kind of fun, you know? I mean, they was after what I had to offer, and I had it for sale, and it was all . . . well, like nothing bad about it."

"And this?" Nell said.

"Well, I hope it was worth while, Miss Nell, helps get you the time you need." Ina took a gulp of her brandy. "Taking them on board, that wasn't anything much, same things going in and out and all. But . . . they wasn't, most of them, even that interested in what they was doing, not in the usual way. It was you being there, it was that they'd made you come up with that to please them, that was what was the big thing for them. They was fucking you, not me." She looked at Nell with brimming eyes. "I've got used to being a whore, but that crowd made me feel like a piece of shit!" She burst into tears.

"It's okay, Ina, it's okay," Nell said, leaning forward and patting the girl on the back as she sobbed. She took Ina into her arms and stroked her back gently.

"Nice," Ina said, her voice muffled against Nell's shoulder. Nell increased the pressure of her stroke, her hand sliding against the silk. Ina shuddered a little and pressed closer against Nell. Nell's hand moved to Ina's side, then to the opening of the wrapper, and inside.

"Nice," Ina repeated fervently.

Ain't the way I go most of the time, Nell thought, but it makes a change. And Ina's earned whatever kind of comforting she craves. Her hand moved down and pulled apart the belt that fastened Ina's wrapper.

Chapter 16

"Hold it right there, mister!"

Faro staggered to a halt and stared at the shape in front of him. By the skirt he could discern it was a woman; the sticklike protrusion extending toward him was most likely a rifle barrel. He realized vaguely that he could not make out more details, because the figure was only dimly illuminated by the rising moon.

It seemed a hell of a lot longer ago than eight or nine hours since he'd seen the last of his companions being hauled away, yet it was only moonrise; he should have been walking until at least dawn by this time. . . . Then fragments of memory came to him, of walking until dark, then through the night, the toolcase that he refused to abandon hanging ever more heavily from his arm, stumbling until dawn, then seeking shelter against the heat of the day in a cool hollow, then getting up and moving on, and by now three parts asleep on his feet. . . .

"No harm meant, ma'am," he croaked. "Been, uh . . . lost my . . ." He could not form the reassuring words he wanted to. "If you . . ." He gestured with his free hand, then saw the woman and the ground she stood on rise up suddenly. His face hit the ground, and he accepted unconsciousness with gratitude.

Half an hour later, he was awake again, though barely, drinking coffee and chewing on a biscuit slathered with cold gravy. "Thanks, ma'am," he said. "Brings me back to life, that does. I been walking since I can't remember, and I guess I just got plumb tuckered."

"That you did," the woman said. She was tall, fine-boned, blonde, with once-fair skin darkened by the sun. "I heard a thrashing in the brush, thought it might be a coyote come to take one of the pigs, and went out to kill it or drive it off. When I saw a man coming toward me, I figured I'd have to do the same thing. Then you keeled over, and I found myself dragging you in here and seeing if I could wake you up. Interesting way to spend the middle of the night." Faro now noticed that she was wearing a cotton nightdress which, while commodious, suggested that what it covered would—for a man with the capacity and interest—be worth uncovering. He yawned, gaping uncontrollably.

"I think I been walking asleep the last hour or so," he said, and took another gulp of coffee. That, and the woman's presence, seemed to be preserving a tiny bubble of awareness, while most of his body seemed to have voted for unconsciousness. "Walking from . . . I ain't sure just where . . . to . . . Listen, I personally am Faro Blake, and I thank you for the coffee and biscuit and the not shooting me, and I will tell you all about it in the morning, and I am just now about to fall over out of this chair onto the floor, and no coffee with the power to pull me out of it. Apologies, ma'am."

"Hang on a second, Mr. Blake," the woman said.

She rose and disappeared from his blurring vision. He was aware of motion and rustling at his side, then a hand on his shoulder. "Blankets and a straw tick on the floor alongside you, just ease yourself down," the woman said. "I'm Con Seeley; wonder if you'll remember that in the morning."

Waking up, with the sun almost overhead, he did. His memory was aided by the sharp smell of fresh coffee, which had been the last sensation lingering in his brain as sleep had claimed him. He looked around and found that he was in a one-room cabin, sparsely furnished but clean, its dirt floor carefully swept. Con Seeley was at the wood stove beginning to cook something in a frying pan. She was dressed in a faded shirt and jeans. Faro was startled, but admired the contours of haunch and leg the pants revealed. He had been in no condition to appreciate such things the night before, but sleep had sharpened his eye.

Faro stirred, and Con Seeley turned. "Coffee's ready now, food soon. I've got the morning chores done, and I'm making lunch. It'll be breakfast for you, but I expect that'll be all right. Pork chops, fried potatoes, some greens I picked."

"Be just fine, thanks," Faro said. He was aware that he was almightily hungry. The cooked beef he had carried had lasted only a day, and he had been over twenty-four hours without eating. He eased himself up from the floor, aching from the effects of his seemingly endless walking, the last stretch of it in such a haze that he now had no idea where he was.

Con Seeley gave him a partial answer to that question when she said, "River's about a hundred feet out the back, if you want to go wash up. With that walking you talked of last night, it might do you good to soak your feet, too."

Faro stepped outside the cabin and looked around. A little distance off was a weathered barn; a cow and some pigs stood or lay in their enclosures; chickens scratched in the yard. A small cornfield and a vegetable garden were close to the house; a little further off was a modestly sized wheat field. The place was located on a strip of land between the bluff of the riverbank and the river itself, toward which he now walked.

Here—wherever here was—the Colorado ran clear and, though not placidly, showed no boiling rapids of the kind he had seen on his last view of it. At the edge there was a pool where the current eddied quietly. He eased his boots off, and peeled away his socks, which seemed almost to have grown to the skin, then rolled up his trousers and sat on the ground, letting his feet into the water. He fingered the growing crop of bristles on his chin and debated returning to his tool case for his razor. But cold-water shaving had never, in his experience, proved comfortable, and the beard might yet prove to be a worthwhile disguise.

The liquid chill soothed the burning away, and he relaxed and lit a cheroot and lay back, squinting against the glare of the sun. When it was done, he rose, refreshed, picked up the boots and stiff socks and padded barefoot back to the cabin. The scent of frying pork grew stronger as he approached, and he quickened his steps.

Over the meal, he told Con Seeley something of his adventures. "That's a lot to have gone through," she said. "I wonder you made it."

"I ain't yet," Faro said. "Yuma's still a ways away."

In turn Con Seeley told him her story. Her widowed father, a prospector, had had no family to leave her with when she was small and had brought her with him on his expeditions. He had suspected the presence of gold in this area and established a claim. To support them while working it, he had planted the comparatively fertile bottom land with a few crops, then brought in some animals. No worthwhile ore ever appeared, but the habit of farming had grown on him, and in time become his sole occupation.

"We raised enough to feed us, and once in a while something over to go to town and trade for what we couldn't grow," Con Seeley said. "After he died, a few years back, I just kept on." She stopped there, leaving unspoken what was clear to Faro, that the place was so remote she couldn't sell it and move on, and that it was a damned lonely existence.

"You get to town often?" he asked.

Con Seeley shrugged. "About twice a year. It's almost thirty miles, and I've only got a mule to draw the wagon I haul in what I've got to trade. But it does me good, once I'm there, seeing other people, buying what I can."

Faro found himself curious. Thirty miles was a long day's journey, and he doubted that whatever Con Seeley had to sell would buy a night's lodging or so plus what she needed to purchase. "Stay with a friend there, do you?" he asked.

She nodded. "Friends. Usually a different one each time."

"Know a lot of people there, do you?"

"I meet them. Go to the saloon, pick out a decent-looking man, let him buy me a drink, then we talk. After we've talked a while, he's usually willing to offer me a bed for the night. His. Mr. Blake," Con Seeley said, looking at his surprised expression, "I don't see a human being, let alone a man, for months at a time, out here. It's how I live, and I'm used to it, but I need a change now and then. And I'm young and I'm healthy. I don't have a man of my own, so I do some borrowing.''

Faro chewed the last of his pork chop and watched her as she rose and removed her dish from the table. Rested and fed, he found the motion of her hips in the tight jeans highly interesting, and the vibration of her breasts under the loose shirt hardly less so. It was not all that many days since he had been with Doll Falkayne, but the events of those days seemed to have occupied a lifetime. The slow stirring in his groin seemed like a reminder of boyhood days rather than a common sensation.

Con Seeley returned to the table and took his plate. As she leaned over for it, Faro had an excellent view of the reasons for the pleasant movements under her shirt. Below the suntanned Vee at her neck, her breasts were full and white; he had a brief view of a brownish nipple before she straightened. He felt his bare toes curl.

"You're quiet," she said. "Did what I said shock you?"

"No," Faro said. "Just . . . You said you'd finished the morning chores. Have to get at the afternoon ones just yet?"

"No. Why?"

"Probably a long time since you been to town, a long time since you'll get to go again, thass all.''

"What . . . oh. You're pretty direct about it, aren't you?"

"Seem like a direct kind of woman to me, you do," Faro said.

Con Seeley looked at the narrow bed that lay against one wall and laughed. "This'll be the first time anything like that's happened here," she said. She unbuttoned her shirt and shrugged out of it, then hung it on the back of a chair. She sat and removed her boots, stood and unfastened her jeans, pushed them down and stepped out of them.

Faro, rapidly undressing, stared at her. She was lean, sinewy, with well-defined stomach muscles, and the generous breasts set high on a broad rib cage. Below her taut belly, a wide patch of wheat-colored hair tapered to the junction of her firm thighs. Her forearms and hands, like her face and neck, were tanned, the rest of her body pale. Her hands were large in proportion to her body, and roughened and worn.

Aware of his inspection, she grinned and said, "Farm woman's body. Not what you'd get with a town lady, but I think you'll find it'll do." She looked at him, her gaze centering on the shaft of flesh that probed the air in front of him. "So'll you."

Faro moved to her, took her arm, and started toward the bed. After a step, she halted and said, "I've got a better idea." She took the rolled-up bedding he had used from the floor and stepped to the doorway. "Come on."

Outside, Faro flinched at the bite of the sun, then relished its warmth on his body. Broken by the trees in the yard, it was far different from the harsh force that had made the last days a misery. Con Seeley set the bedding down in the yard and lay on it, legs drawn up.

"Fine with me," Faro said, "but how come out here's better than in there?"

"This farm's all I've got," Con Seeley said. "And I'm all it's got—we're part of each other, I help it grow, it gives me what I need to live. This now, I want it to be where I can feel the farm."

Smell it, too, Faro thought, as a breeze came to him from where the cow was tethered. Well, hell, no harm ever come from catering to a lady's notions in this line.

He lowered himself to her and stroked her breasts, enjoying as always the stiffening of the nipples. Con Seeley reached down and took hold of his erection, pulling it to the moist convolutions between her legs, and clamping her thighs around his waist. Not one for the appetizers, then, Faro thought, and drove into her.

Con Seeley panted with each thrust, mouth agape with pleasure and eyes staring past him into the sky. Her breasts spread under the pressure of his chest, and the muscles of her belly tensed and relaxed in time to the movements of her body, matched to his thrusts.

Oh, shit, I'm going to come in no time atall, Faro thought, and it'll be all over before she's had half the good of it. Then he caught sight of the cow staring at him with what seemed to be dumb wonder, and the satirical glance of the pigs peering from their pen, and the sudden tide of orgasmic urgency subsided.

From time to time, Faro tried to introduce a variation or so into the session, but, wordlessly, Con Seeley let him know that she wanted things to continue as they were. After what seemed like a very long time, he sensed that she was building up to her climax, but that his own could be a long time off.

"Charawk!"

Faro jumped as a curious chicken, investigating this unprecedented phenomenon in its territory, pecked at his buttock. Under him, Con Seeley responded to the change in movement with a vigorous motion of her own; and in a moment, both had come, and lay contentedly sprawled on the bedding, now moist with the sweat of their exertions.

Faro, breathing deeply, stroked Con Seeley's full breast, brushing his fingers over the now-flaccid nipple. "You know how to milk?" she said.

Faro withdrew his hand rapidly. "Huh?"

"Could use some help with the chores," Con Seeley said.

At supper, after having done what a man used to considering operating a faro dealing box as manual labor could do in the way of assisting in farming tasks, Faro said, "Listen, I got to be getting on. Is that town you go to honest to God the nearest place there is around here where I could get a horse?"

Con Seeley nodded silently.

"Well, I wonder if . . . See, I got some money on me, and . . . if you could see your way to making a special trip, I could, like, see you wouldn't lose by it. I mean, I ain't up to walking that far."

Con Seeley looked at him. "You know," she said, "you're not a bad hand at the work that has to be done here. You could learn, anyhow. Between us, we could feed ourselves and have a little over, and live here, and . . ."

Faro shook his head. "Honored you'd ask, ma'am," he said. "But it ain't my way of living, and there it is. I am out of my element here, gratifying though some of the circumstances is."

"Of course," Con Seeley said with a sigh. "I knew that, knew you'd be on your way. But if I hadn't asked, I'd have felt like a damned fool afterwards, just in case I might have been wrong about that. Yes, I could take you to town, but I doubt it would do you much good. The livery stable doesn't have much beyond crowbaits, and it'd put you miles out of your way. The best thing is the river."

"I ain't heard no steamboats whistling for a landing since I been here," Faro said.

"No, they don't come by on any schedule any more. But the river's not bad from here down to Yuma, as far as I've heard. It's shallow, and there's some sandbars, but nothing worse. My dad used to put together a raft and float on down some distance, when he wanted to look into a strike he'd heard about, and I know how to do it. You could be in Yuma in a couple or three days, probably, if you did that, and no walking or horseback riding involved."

Faro considered the idea. He had never rafted, which was one thing against it. On the other hand, he had ridden and walked a good deal lately, and found both to be pure hell, which were two things in favor. And, with the river shallower and less intemperate down here and for the rest of the way, the dangers couldn't be all that great.

"Okay, I'll appreciate that. You show me how to put one of them things together tomorrow, and I'll be on my way."

That night, Con Seeley's bed had its first usage for any purpose other than sleep. And Con Seeley learned a number of things about the usage of her body. "When I get to town next," she murmured drowsily, "there'll be a surprise or so for whoever gives me lodging. I never knew about that."

"Out on your ownsome, how would you?" Faro said. "And then there's this. . . ."

Putting together a raft under Con Seeley's direction was simpler than Faro had expected, though calling for some exertion in the felling and trimming of the trees that grew along the river bank. By midmorning, he had lashed together the logs he had cut with rope scavenged from the barn, and cut a long pole to assist in the navigation of the craft.

"Pole out to the center and keep there," Con Seeley advised. "I haven't heard of rapids below here, but if you see any ahead, push in for shore and see if you can work it along 'til you're past them. If you see a sandbar ahead, make sure to keep to the deepwater side of it. If you go aground, you can usually push off with the poles. Or when you're close to Yuma, the tides from the Gulf come up that far and past, and you can wait and float free sometimes. Now get on your way."

Faro placed his battered tool case and the flour sack of provisions Con Seeley had pressed on him in the center of the raft, pushed off, and turned to wave at her. She was walking up the path to the cabin, not looking behind her.

Faro lay on his back, looking at the late afternoon sky, and taking bites of cold ham between puffs at his cheroot. This is the way to travel, for sure. The feet don't take a beating, nor the ass, and there ain't even that eternal clickety-clack and cinders you get on the railroad. Just drift on down, let the river do the work.

Just before dark, he thought, I better work in toward shore and put up for the night. Warm out, so's I won't feel the want of blankets. That can wait a while, though. Nice to just lie here and watch the shore go by, slow and easy.

Not so slow as it was, though, come to think of it. That cottonwood over there kind of whipped by. . . . Faro sat up and looked ahead. Downriver, a boil of white water surrounded a fang of rock protruding from the surface of the river. There was plenty of open water to the far side of it, but the raft was on the near side. Faro probed for the bottom with the pole, found it, and pushed, trying to get the raft well clear of the obstruction.

The raft bucked in the increasing current, throwing him off balance. He flung his arms wide to keep steady, and the pole was wrenched from his grasp, falling into the water. It floated for a moment, maddeningly close but out of reach, beside the raft. Faro was, he saw, now headed directly for the jagged rock.

He closed his eyes briefly as it hit, shuddered, scraped past, and was then again racing downstream. Don't know how we got through that, he thought. Then he found his footing becoming unsteady and looked down. Loose rope flapped at the edge of the raft, and the logs under his feet were working apart. The contact with the rock must have cut the ropes that had lashed the raft together, and it would only be a matter of minutes before it turned into a collection of kindling floating downstream.

Faro grabbed his tool case, and swore as his bag of provisions slid into the widening gap between two logs and was lost. Then his foot slipped into a similar gap, and he was in the water, in danger of being crushed between the floating logs. He dove beneath the surface, holding his breath, and one-handed—it never occurred to him to drop the tool case—swam as best he could for the near shore. Surfacing, when he thought he was free of the remnants of the raft, was harder than he had expected; his clothes had absorbed all the water they could, and were weighing him down.

He sank again as one of the last of the logs that had comprised the raft struck him a stunning blow on the head, but he continued, dazed, to make for the shore.

With the last of his strength, he clawed his way onto it, then collapsed face down, his legs still tugged at by the current of the river.

Chapter 17

Faro came awake with mud in his mouth and a stabbing pain in his head. I can count on the fingers of one foot the times it's been a pleasure to wake up lately, he thought.

He pushed himself upright and looked around. His tool case lay ahead of him on the rock shore. He was in a dense stand of reeds, a couple of them crushed by the pressure of his face where he had fallen. The sun was up, but still low, painting the far shore of the river with vivid light. I been out for twelve hours, anyhow, he thought. Does that count as sleep, or being coldcocked by that damn log? He moved and found it more difficult than he had anticipated; his clothes felt like a gritty suit of armor. A little investigation showed him that they had become packed with sand and mud in the course of his escape from the broken-up raft.

Sighing and cursing, he stripped, and gathered his bundled garments to rinse them. A sharp stone on the bank bit into the arch of his left foot, and he jumped, tripped and fell forward. His clothes were jolted from his arms and dropped into the river. He hopped, rubbing his aching foot, and stared in incredulous rage as they bobbed briefly on the rushing water, then sank out of sight.

Faro took a deep breath and, walking carefully, returned to his only possessions, his tool case and his boots. Well, here I am, naked and God knows how far from Yuma, yes, that's where I am. That's where Faro Blake's cleverness has got him to, yes sir.

He spent a satisfying but unproductive five minutes in invoking the direst punishments that Jehovah, Satan, or any other being with the power to make things hot for anyone, could inflict on Sam Volksmacht, Three-Balls Tabard, and about anybody else he had ever known. Spent, he contemplated his boots and case moodily. After a moment, he brightened. Opening the case, he inspected it. To his surprise—one bit of good luck—it had proven to be almost watertight, and the contents were not, as he had feared, ruined. More to the immediate point, his flask of bourbon was intact, and almost half-full.

He took a good pull at it, and then another. A man that's naked and afoot and lost, he told himself, that man might as well be drunk to boot. Got nothing to lose.

By the time the flask was empty, Faro was beginning to find his predicament humorous. I strike out, wearing boots and bare skin, carrying the case, maybe folks'll take me for something new in the line of a traveling salesman. Good afternoon, sir or madam, I'm here to demonstrate our latest invisible clothing.

He was exploring this fancy, dimly aware that it was the only way to avoid thinking about what to do next, a prospect he did not care for at all, when he heard a laugh, not far distant.

He forced his wits together and listened. Another laugh, definitely a woman's, then the sound of voices. He moved cautiously along through the reeds next to the river bank, and heard the voices grow louder. He carefully parted a stand of reeds and looked through.

Clothes and sheets were spread out to dry on the turf of the riverbank. A brief memory of the Indian woman Walsh and Emmett had encountered in the foothills of the Blacks came to Faro. Three women splashed in the shallows of the river, dressed as Faro was, two of them short, dark and plump, one taller, fairer and with fiery red hair. The tall one, in water to her knees, tossed a rubber ball to one of her companions, who fired it rapidly at the other, who returned it.

"You're catching on, Ana," the fair girl called. "We'll have you pitching for the baseball team soon."

"Oo, *señorita*," Ana squealed, "I can' play ball with all those men!"

"You do plenty of playing already, though not the same kind, far as I hear," the *"señorita"* said drily.

In Faro's bemused state, this struck him as the height of wit, and he guffawed. The two dark girls shrieked and ran off, dropping the ball. The fair one stiffened, looked toward the clothes on the bank, then directly to where Faro lay behind the reeds. "All right, you've seen what there is to see by now," she said. "I won't bother to cover up. Come out and explain what you're doing on Schiff land, spying on Schiff women. And if you've got any ideas about—oh."

Faro stepped through the reeds. "In the same case as yourself, ma'am," he said with alcoholic amiability. "Only my clothes has gone down the river, whiles yours is already for the putting on whenas you want, see?" He chuckled and sank to squat on the shore.

The red-haired girl looked at him for a long moment, then came over and sat next to him. "This is the strangest conversation I ever had, me and a man jaybird-naked, but you've got me curious. How'd your clothes come to be drifting down the river?"

"There was this rock, see," Faro said. "And I stepped on it and I dropped them in, and, whoosh, there they went."

"Why'd you have them off in the first place?"

"'Cause they was full of sand and mud from when the raft broke up."

"The raft?"

"That I took on down here after the farm that I got to when the cowpokes took my . . . Listen, ma'am, it's a damned long story, and I have got a knock on the head, and the best part of a pint of bourbon inside me, and I am enough out of things so that it don't strike me as strange that I'm sitting next to a handsome woman and neither of us with a stitch amongst us, and no notice taken. Can you give me the lend of a sheet or whatever, and a place to rest up at?"

"Sure," said the girl—who was, as Faro, even in his blurred state, had noticed, strikingly good-looking. "My pa's a good Bible man, believes in feeding the hungry and clothing the naked. Though I don't suppose he's had just the kind of opportunity you present before." She went to the clothes spread on the bank, pulled a dress over her head, and returned to Faro, carrying a shirt and a pair of breeches.

After he had retrieved his tool case and boots from the reeds, and the girl—Flame Schiff was her name, she told him—had coaxed the two servant girls from the woods and into their clothes, Faro was transported in the comparative luxury of a mule cart carrying the girls and the laundry to the Schiff ranch house, two miles distant. After being introduced to the patriarch—with no mention of the precise circumstances of the meeting with his daughter, especially the costuming of the event, though Ana and Elvira were taken with a fit of the giggles—Faro was bustled up to a spare bedroom, where he managed to strip off his borrowed clothes and fall into a deep sleep.

"Incredible," Jacob Schiff said. "To trail an outlaw to his den and attack him, for the sake of a woman. It is like the old stories I remember reading in the *gymnasium*. And then what happened?"

Sitting at dinner with the rancher, his foreman, some of the senior hands, and Flame Schiff, Faro expanded on his story. Without Flame's presence, he would have provided some details which he was sure his male hearers would have appreciated. From her casual unconcern about her own nakedness and his, he suspected that she would have appreciated them as well, but social decorum demanded that he disregard that, at least in mixed company.

"Well, old Tabard told us what he'd do to us, which we hadn't taken into account ahead of time, so a dozen of us figured we'd best strike out for Yuma, to get out of his range, and follow the Colorado. And we . . ."

When Faro finished his narrative, Jacob Schiff shook his head. "Incredible, I say again. Yet I believe you. The fates seem to have worked against you, yet you have come through, that is remarkable."

"Only me, though," Faro said. "It galls me that I lost the rest."

"From what you say, they lost themselves, or had bad luck you could do nothing about," Jacob Schiff said. "And it may be that all are not lost. I know Sonnenschein from the old country, we came here together in '48, young men. He's tough but fair. If your friends had a chance to tell what happened, they might yet live."

"Hope so," Faro said.

"Now," Jacob Schiff said. "You are almost to where you want to be, Yuma. A dreadful place, but no matter, that is your goal. Very well. I have business interests there, and I keep a coach to take mail in and bring it out to me; it is no more than eight hours' drive, on a good track. I am sending it in tonight; if you wish, you may be on it, and arrive at Yuma for breakfast."

Faro goggled at him, taken totally aback. After the last ten years, or ten days, or whatever it had been, the prospect of actually finishing his journey was startling. It had come to seem a given condition of his life that he would always be on the way, never arriving. "Uh . . . sure, sir. And many thanks."

"Your story has repaid any favor I can do you," Schiff said. "If you are still weary, I suggest that you take a few hours' sleep before the coach leaves."

As Faro made his way to the stairs leading to his room, Flame Schiff came up to him in the hall and laid her hand on his arm. "You didn't tell everything about how we met this morning," she said.

"Well, no," Faro said. "Figured your pa might get his Dutch up or so, the idea of me and you jaybirding it together, though there wasn't no harm to it."

"I wonder if you told him everything about the other things that happened," Flame Schiff said. "Miss Falkayne and Miss Seeley must be very nice women, to have helped you the way you say they did."

"They was . . . is," Faro said.

"And you told everything there was to tell about the time you spent with them?" Flame Schiff said.

"Uh . . . you got to sort of pick what you say, otherwise the story'd take forever to tell," Faro said uneasily.

"Huh." Flame Schiff looked at him. "Well, you'd best get your couple of hours' sleep before pa's coach takes you in to Yuma. Myself, I'm not that tired. Hot,

moonlight nights like this, I sometimes get Ana and
Elvira up, and we sneak out to a little creek out back of
the house a way, and splash and swim and play, the
way we were doing this morning. It cuts into sleep
some, and we're tired the next day, but it's worth it for
the fun."

"I ain't had any splashing and swimming fun in quite
a while," Faro said after a thoughtful pause. "Seeing
as there ain't no news in what's to be seen for any
concerned, after this morning, wonder if I could keep
you ladies company?"

Flame Schiff smiled. "An hour from now, out back.
We'll show you the way."

"You bigger now than this morning, *señor*," Elvira
giggled, snaking her hand under the water to Faro's
midsection.

"'Cause you're closer than you was this morning,"
Faro said. He caught the girl by her plump buttocks
and upended her; her back and head splashed, scattering the reflections of the moon in the placid waters of
the creek. From behind, Ana's legs were around his
and her plump breasts squashed moistly against his
back. He clutched Elvira to him, sliding easily into
her, moving her as close to him as he could, then
pushing her away and pulling her back again. She
grinned up at him in the moonlight, paddling with her
arms to keep her head above water.

Flame Schiff sat, half submerged, at the edge of the
water, looking on, a smile visible on her face. "Hoo!"
Elvira said, convulsing. "My turn now," Ana said
over Faro's shoulder. "You still got any left?"

"Plenty," Faro said. This was splashing and swimming fun for sure, but, with Flame Schiff waiting, he
was making the effort to hold back until he could get to
her. The coach would leave pretty soon, and there

wouldn't be time for him to renew himself once he had come. Elvira had been easy enough to bring off; he hoped Ana would prove the same.

Ana led him to the edge of the creek, close to where Flame Schiff sat, and bestrode him, wet breasts bobbing as she moved. Elvira sprawled on the other side of them, breathing contentedly.

Ana moved faster, then faster yet, and said, "Ai!" and bent backwards, mouth open, staring at the sky. After a moment, she shuddered and said, "Now, *la señorita.*"

"Yes," Flame Schiff said. "I can hardly wait for it."

"Nor can't I," Faro said weakly, having thought about all the distressing things he could to keep from coming during Ana's last wild gyration. On balance, he supposed it was the rattler doing for Brown that had worked most effectively.

Flame Schiff inched her way up the bank and lay back on her elbows. Elvira and Ana moved to her and stroked her legs, then parted them. Each girl then shifted backward, cushioning their mistress's back with their bodies, and caressed her shoulders and breasts. Faro moved to her, and felt himself taken by the two girls' hands and guided in. With the three women's faces, one slack with the solemnity of passion, two gleeful with satisfaction and mischief, looking at him, he felt as if his erection had swollen to twice its size, and was being enfolded twice as tightly as before.

Flame Schiff turned slowly, rhythmically, under him, the moonlight in her eyes; Faro's hands moved to her breasts, joining fingers with Ana and Elvira, stroking, kneading the nipples, then lightly slapping as the pace of their movements quickened.

There was the feeling of something turning inside

Flame Schiff, and she stiffened under him, giving a sharp cry.

As the coach started for Yuma, just at midnight, Faro raised his hat—borrowed, as was the rest of his gear—to Flame Schiff and her father, standing in front of the ranch house. From an upper window, Ana and Elvira waved vigorously. He sank back in the coach seat and closed his eyes. If I don't get some sleep on this trip, he thought, they might just as well stop the coach in front of the undertaker's and offload me there.

Chapter 18

The jolting of the coach did not disturb Faro's sleep during the eight-hour journey to Yuma, and he awoke to find himself being driven through the early-morning streets of the town. He stared wonderingly at the buildings that passed by the coach's windows. It was only a few months back that he had seen them, but it might have been in another life. Over the last days, he had come to accept that he would never see a familiar place again, and it took some getting used to.

Let off at Schiff's town office, he stood and pondered what to do next, and decided it would best be worked out over breakfast. He found the nearest saloon and ordered his preferred morning fare, the egg beaten up in brandy.

Best thing, I go 'round to Nell's place, he finally decided. He fingered the beard on his chin and took a glance at the clothes that Jacob Schiff had provided and grinned. Likely she won't recognize me. Be fun to come in as a customer and see how long can I fool her.

182

The first test of his unintended disguise came upon his arrival at Nell Garvin's establishment. To his surprise, there were a number of loungers on her front porch, even at this early hour. And even more surprising, he recognized some of the men he had played poker against when he was last in Yuma—Barber, the banker, Mosby, the fellow who was raking it in over feeding the unlucky fellows on Prison Hill, and others. What they—what anybody—was doing here at this hour was beyond him.

In any case, as he mounted the steps, he received only curious glances, but no start of recognition or any hail by name. A white fluffball darted from the front door, opened against the heat, and sank needlelike teeth in his leg. At least that little bitch Claire knows me, Faro thought angrily, though I don't see as it does me much good. The brief howl he gave amused the men on the porch, and he glowered at them as he entered the door.

Inside the house, he asked a chore girl he did not recognize, "Miz Garvin in?"

"Yes," she said, applying a duster to the ornate glass shade of a lamp.

"Like to see her."

"Oh. All right, I'll get her in. Expect you're another of them," she said, looking at him with dislike.

Another of which? Faro wondered, looking after the departing woman.

He braced himself to start a conversation with Nell which would wind up in the revelation of his identity; that would be a laugh all around, for sure.

Nell Garvin entered the front parlor and said, "Given up shaving, Blake? Go on a few more years that way, and you'll look like President Hayes."

"Shit, I didn't think you'd know me, Nell," Faro said. "Other folks that's seen me before didn't."

"Any time, any place, Blake," Nell said, "whiskers or not. Oh, Blake, I am so damned glad to see you!"

For the first time since he had known her, Nell Garvin rushed to him, threw her arms about him, pushed her face into his shoulder, and began to heave and dampen his borrowed coat with her tears.

"Well, my ten thousand'll get you off the hook, from what you say," Faro said, after Nell had explained her situation. "So I'll just go down and get it out of that box."

"You'd do that?" Nell said.

"Well, I guess," Faro said. He had no idea why, but it seemed clear that he would.

"I never meant that serious," Nell said. "I was just stalling those fellows out there, hoping something would turn up. But it ain't. I don't know what to do."

"Take the money and pay off," Faro said.

Nell patted his hand. "No. That'd just take care of things for a little while. They'd come up with something else, and it'd work out the same, only you'd be out your money. I got to think of something that'll get them off my back for good."

"Well, I been doing some planning and such, a good bit above what I ever done before," Faro said, "and maybe I can figure out what should be done here. Lemme tell you about all that."

"Well," Nell Garvin said, "I can see you've got some seasoning now in the planning line. But that don't change the fact that I got one more day before I'm out of business unless I can pay up. And I don't propose to do that with your money."

"Uh," Faro said. "Well, a good, ripe plan like what this calls for, that usually takes a week or more. But maybe I can come up with one fast. Lemme think on it."

Thinking, Faro stalked the streets of Yuma, ignoring the oppressive heat, and occasionally cursing as he smacked a mosquito that had settled on his neck or wrists. Two or three ideas occurred to him, but they fell apart when examined, or required capable assistance. He kicked a stone and watched it raise puffs of dust, then looked up and spoke in surprise. "Hey, Phil."

Slick Phil Bowyer raised a finger to his derby. "Blake. New duds, eh? Would hardly have known you."

"What the hell happened up there? Thought you were for the rope, but there wasn't nothing I could do about it, once those fellows had you, and me with my horse run off," Faro said.

Bowyer shrugged. "The hands came up, took us in, told us we were to hang. But they took us to old man Sonnenschein first, thank God, him liking to have a hand in everything that goes on on his spread. And once we got to him, I told him the tale, and he let up."

"What kind of story'd you tell him?" Faro asked.

"For once, the truth," Slick Phil Bowyer said. "I'm not used to it, but it was stranger than anything I could make up, which is why it worked with him, I guess. He could see we didn't know enough about cows to be rustlers, and when we offered to pay whatever he wanted for the damn beast, he relented."

"And you did that?" Faro asked.

Slick Phil Bowyer grinned. "Four times what it was worth, as far as I can estimate. But then, when we all got to be pals, we stayed on, and Toad Dabney won the whole thing back at poker, and a good bit beyond. Old man Sonnenschein sent us down here with some of his people that had business here; just got in yesterday and aiming to leave tomorrow. The others have already scattered, and glad to be able to. Hey, I ran into Blinky Castle; Sam stood him train fare down here before he and Elena cut out. Told him some of what we'd been through, and he's putting it into a song. Listen, Blake, I was damned well wrong about butchering that cow. That nearly got our necks stretched, never mind how it finally came out, and I shouldn't have gone up against you about it. You have my apologies."

Faro had been thinking as Slick Phil Bowyer talked. "No need," he said. "I was damned hungry myself. But, listen, you feel you got something to make up to me, I got a proposition to put to you."

At about one o'clock, a small, dapper man in a derby and the bearded stranger the loungers on the porch had noticed in the morning strode up the steps to Nell Garvin's front porch. "Gents," the bearded man said in a hoarse voice. "Understand we're all in the same boat, creditors to the lady of the house."

"I've got her note of hand for a thousand dollars," the dapper man said. "And I'm here to get it, or whatever's left after she's sold up."

"Me too," the bearded man croaked.

Howard Barber laughed. "Welcome to the fraternity," he said. "I've no idea if the lady can pay off her debts, but if she doesn't, there'll be enough to go around, I don't doubt." He consulted his watch. "About time to go inside and partake of our hostess's bounty. Give her credit, she puts on a good lunch and supper, and other diversions. That's the only way she's kept afloat so far, but that's about at an end, so let's enjoy it while we can. When we own the place, I doubt we'll be so generous to ourselves."

After the lunch, which was all that Barber had said it would be, the creditors settled themselves in the parlor. The dapper man proposed to pass the hot hours of the afternoon with a few hands of poker and was seconded enthusiastically by the others.

"I tell you," the bearded man said, "I'll stake my note of hand that I have of Miz Garvin. I ain't sure she's going to be good for it, and maybe some of you gentlemen would care to have a sporting flutter at it."

The dapper man sneered. "I'll play for cash, not paper," he said. But the bearded man persisted, and the creditors, seeing a chance for a larger slice of the pie they were cutting up, joined in. The dapper man called for fresh cards, which Nell's chore girl supplied, and dealt the first hand.

The betting was light, with only cash in, the notes and obligations on Nell Garvin each player held being reserved for later, heavier play by mutual agreement.

"Mine, I think," the dapper man said, laying down three kings, a jack and a five and reaching for the pot. "Anybody got cards to beat that?"

Amid a general shaking of heads around the table, the bearded man said, "Not quite. Looks like my hand don't beat yours, but it's interesting all the same." He laid down a pair of kings, a six, seven and trey.

"Thought I seen you palm a card," the bearded man said. "Now, you fourflusher—"

The dapper man clawed at his vest; the bearded man drew a short-barrelled gun, aimed and fired. The dapper man shrieked and fell over backwards, clutching his chest, and lay sprawled on the floor, blood spilling from his mouth, staring blindly at the ceiling.

"He reached first, you saw that," the bearded man said gruffly. Powder smoke hung in the air. "Now, less go on playing. Agreed you're staking your notes on this place next hand, right? I'll claim that fellow's since I doubt he's got heirs about. You all ante yours up. Your deal, I think," he said to Barber.

The shaken creditors looked at the body on the floor and at the bearded man who sat calmly at the table.

"Ah . . . I think we want to have a discussion about that," Howard Barber said.

"Discuss what you want, so long's you play or fold," the bearded man said, his hand resting casually on his weapon.

"There's more of us than him," Asa Mosby whispered urgently, when the creditors had withdrawn to one side of the room. "We don't have to—"

"We're over a barrel," Howard Barber said. He glanced at the still form of the dapper man on the floor. "We could take that fellow, sure, but not 'til he'd killed one of us or more, the way he did that one. And then what? The ones that's left would have to go into court and explain how come we were in a shooting scrape in a whorehouse. You want to figure how that's going to set with the people we deal with, our wives and such?"

"Seems like we'd best fold," Carson said. "Don't know what cards that man holds, but the ironware he's got his hand on is a pretty good convincer. I'd say we've had all the good out of this deal that we're going to, and it's time to forget it. I'll talk to the City Hall people about that tax stuff, too. If that hardcase is going to be taking over our interests, I'd as soon not make an enemy out of him."

When the formalities of handing over the notes and obligations were completed, the creditors left, studiously ignoring the body on the floor.

"Gone now," the bearded man said after a few moments. The dapper man arose, wiped the drying blood from his mouth with a handkerchief, and said,

"The old cackle-bladder always does it, Blake. Bite down on it, let some chicken blood spill out, and the marks think you're corpsed on the spot."

"Worked okay," Faro said. "Obliged to you, Phil." He opened the cylinder of his Reid's .38 and substituted live cartridges for the blanks it had held for the performance.

Slick Phil Bowyer moved to the door, which the existing creditors had left open behind them. "Hey, listen," he said.

Faro heard the screech of a fiddle from the street, and a quavering voice.

Now, when they came nigh to the turrible canyon,
'Twas Blake that did show 'em the way to come
through. . . .

Blinky was still working on his ballad, then. Wonder if he's right about folks listening to it long after he's gone? Faro pondered.

After Slick Phil left, he sat at the table, looking at the papers he had won for Nell and waiting for her to come in. Everything had worked out fine, after all; she was keeping her place, he had his money and hide intact. So it's time to move on to wherever, I guess. One thing, not to that ghost town, Sulphur. Not this time, anyway.

MATT BRAUN'S

WEST

IS THE REAL WEST!

And a Matt Braun novel
is your guarantee of
authentic western
adventure!

Follow the adventures of
Matt's great western hero
Luke Starbuck—in these
novels you may have missed!

JURY OF SIX	43804/$1.95	___
TOMBSTONE	82033/$1.95	___
HANGMAN'S CREEK	82031/$1.75	___
THE SPOILERS	82034/$1.95	___

··

164